KING OF CHICAGO

A Novel By
SHELLI MARIE
&
MARINA J

Acknowledgements

(Marina J)

I first want to give a major shout out to Ms. Shelli Marie for collaborating with me on this project. You have always been an inspiration to me and it has been an honor to be able to work with you.

Thanks to Leo Sullivan for giving us the opportunity! Much Love!

As always, I have to thank my team ZitrO Publications. Divine and Nkki Ortiz you guys are the best! This year we are going to rock the literary world....they ain't ready. Lol.

To my girls Jerrona and Rachel, we have been through the fire and we have come out unscathed. That just goes to show you that not even the devil could deter us. I love you guys.

Let me not forget my babies, the Super Six. Mommy loves you guys and everything I do; I do it for you all.

To all the readers who continue to support me, it is very, very much appreciated and I will continue to thank each and every one of y'all every chance I get. I now turn things over to my wonderful co-writer.

Thanks for supporting Marina J!

Acknowledgements

(*Shelli Marie*)

To God Almighty I give the glory!

To Leo Sullivan: Thanks for this opportunity to work with you once again. Much Love & It don't stop!

To my family support team:

Jeremy, Jessica, Danielle, and Vassie Jr.

Thanks for all of your encouragement. I love you!

To the rest of the Dishman Klan: Jennifer Dishman, Kim Dishman, Marlo and Devin Dishman,

Daddy and Genora Dishman. I love you all dearly!

To Marina J, I am once again honored that you chose me to do another book with you, especially after I enjoyed writing the first one. I wish you nothing but the best Chica! Nothing but LOVE! Always Sis!

To my extended support team: Special Thanks to My Bae (JC/Jon Criss), Sheila James, Teruka B, TonYelle Reese-Britt, Alexys Price, JeaNida Luckie-Weatherall, Tiarra Neely, Lakeisha Holmes, Denise Henson, Junanya Shiel, thanks for the encouragement and also for always showing me LOVE!!

Thanks for supporting Shelli Marie

Dedications

(Marina J)

This book is dedicated to all my readers. If it were not for all of you then I would not be able to do any of this. You guys ROCK!

Dedications

(*Shelli Marie*)

Marina J, this is for you Sis! Thanks for allowing me to help you share your amazing story! For that, I am grateful...

Nothing but LOVE... Always

SHELLI MARIE & MARINA J

<u>Prologue</u>

Amon Rivers was born on a cold December day in 1982, Christmas day to be exact. That was how Naida knew her son would be special. She told anybody who would listen that he was a gift from God himself seeing as they shared the same birthday. His IQ and genuine curiosity were what made him so unique. His natural ability to do certain things let his mother know that he would be a leader someday. She just did not know how true that would be.

Amon was a very intelligent child. He was so smart that his mother allowed the school to test him. Surprising everyone, his results exceeded even the highest of scores. *Yes, he was a real life genius...* His smarts were immediately compared to that of a well-known African American by the name of Lonnie Johnson. He was definitely gifted.

School was a breeze for Amon and before you knew it, he had finished high school and he was only twelve years old. There were newspaper articles and everything about the kid genius. People were trying to recruit him for college and everything but when his mom, Naida, asked Amon what he wanted to do, he replied with a simple answer. "I just wanna be a kid mom."

PART ONE

THE MAN

Amon Rivers

I was thirteen years old and getting real antsy. I wasn't like other kids. I was a certified mastermind. School was so easy that they wound up testing me up each year. Before I knew it, I was taking my high school exams. Shortly after that, I received my diploma. Yep, ya boy was a high school graduate before I even hit my teenage years.

Once I completed that shit, I pretty much could do whatever I wanted. At that time, college was the last thing on my mind. I was tired of that school shit.

My mom always told me that if I had made it all the way through high school and graduated then she had done her job. I guess she didn't expect me to do that shit at such an early age.

With nothing to do during the day but hang out, I became familiar with the guys in my neighborhood and soon enough I was teaching the local dope boys how to capitalize on their shit. They were some sloppy motherfuckers for real. Some of them were cool taking words from a kid like me but others tried to clown me because they thought I was bullshitting about my accomplishments.

I remember when I met Marco Rivera. He hustled a few blocks over from where I lived in Humboldt Park. I used to see him all the time with his boys stuntin' and shit. I started to watch him for a little while and I noticed how fucked up his operation was. For him to be the "boss" he sure was stupid as hell. I sat there almost the whole day watching the moves he made and by six that evening I decided to approach him. I walked across the street and stepped right up to him.

"You're Marco right?"

"Who wants to know kid?"

"My name's Amon and I wanna be down."

"Ha, can y'all believe this kid? Yo shorty how old are you?"

"I'm 13 and I wanna be down. I think we both could help each other out."

"Check this out shorty. Ain't shit you can help me with because I got this shit on lock."

"Ha, on lock you say? Well I been watching you all day and I saw plenty of inconsistencies with the way you run things."

"Yo', do you know who the fuck I am? You better carry yo ass on before ya mama gotta bury you."

"Who you are doesn't intimidate me. Do you know who the fuck I am? Apparently not, because you obviously look like someone who doesn't know how to read. Anyway, let me get back to what I was doing before I came over here to help your weak ass out. By the way, you should be more careful. There's been an undercover sitting on the corner of Kimball and North Avenue watching your dusty ass since this morning. So much having shit on lock huh?"

I knew I had pissed Marco off, but after I mentioned the undercover, his ass was shook. I didn't give a damn though. The shit was funny to me. That fool wanted to underestimate me so I was going to show his ass how to do shit. I could not stand a flawed motherfucker. Especially one who walked around like his shit didn't stink and he was God or something. That was just how dumb asses like him ended up in jail as somebody's bitch.

After Marco's response, I knew that I would just have to find a way to do shit on my own. It sucked though, because with that nigga there it was definitely some good potential to build a great empire.

I went back home and made me something to eat as I contemplated on how I was going to get some shit popping. Being as smart as I was gave me plenty of opportunities for legit jobs but all that shit was boring.

'Y'all saw how I flew through school.'

Nah, I needed something challenging. Something that would really make me use my brain and be exciting at the same time.

I was in deep thought staring off into space when my cousin, DJ, walked in. He made a sandwich, grabbed some chips and a juice and sat with me.

"What's on ya mind Amon?"

"Just thinking DJ. I'm bored as hell and I wanna make some money. Mama said because of the stupid ass state laws I can't do shit but wait till I'm 15 to get a job. I don't wanna wait. I need money now."

"What you need money for? Ya mama gives you everything and then some."

"Yeah but I want my own money. I'm tired of asking for shit. I wanna feel like a man. What good is being a genius if I can't use that intelligence right now?"

"You got something in mind?"

"I wanna start my own empire."

DJ laughed at me like some shit was funny but stopped when he noticed I was being serious.

"Yo you talking bout drugs cousin?"

"Yeah what else? There's money to be made like that. Tons of money and if it's done right then we could be richer than a muhfucka."

"But we're just a couple kids. What could we possibly do and who would really fuck with us like that?"

"Let me worry about the business side of shit and you worry about how we're gonna get the product."

"Product? Yo you for real ain't you?"

"As real as I can get."

"Aight bet cousin. I'm with you. Just tell me what you need."

I began to run down to DJ what I would need for him to do. By the time I was done explaining shit to him he was more than ready.

Now I had something to do. It was gonna be risky but if I did it just right then it would turn a profit for everybody involved. First order of business would be to get at all the dealers around my way who were considered major players. That was the easy part. Getting them to hear me out just because I was a kid was the hard part but I loved a challenge.

DJ went on about his business as I set my plan in motion. I wanted to be retired by the time I was thirty with more than enough money that my great-grandchildren wouldn't want for nothing. By the time I was done, I was going to be the *King of Chicago.*

Ty'Keisha

I was only sixteen when I started chasing Amon. He was the finest hustler on the streets and he and his cousin DJ were already running shit at a young age. I had already been getting close to the crew just to get close to his ass.

After doing everything possible to get some attention without looking obvious, I finally got him to say more than two words to me. I must admit, my ass was shocked.

"I heard you been scopin' a nigga out," Amon laughed as he tried to clown me in front of his friends.

"You heard right. I ain't shame 'bout mine boo," I hollered back with a smack of my glossed lips.

"Come on over here and let me see how you rockin' those short ass shorts with ya fast ass," he teased pulling me near him. I about lost it.

"Ty, how many of my homeboys you let hit it ma'?" he whispered in my ear as he squeezed my ass tight enough to get me moist below.

"Not one," I answered honestly.

Amon pulled back from me and held my hand in the air.

"Which one of you nigga's done hit this?" he yelled out.

My ass could have pissed my damn pants, but I sucked that shit up and held my head high. I knew that I had pushed up on a few, but not one could say that they even tasted my sweetness.

"Come on now, I ain't gon' be mad. She ain't mine," he smiled then whispered again. "At least not yet. You still have a couple of more tests to pass before I can even consider that shit ma'."

"Aint that a bitch?" I thought silently.

"So Russell, you hit this man? I saw her creeping out ya spot last week. It was kind of late too bruh," Amon blurted as he spit out the shell of a sunflower seed and poured some more into his mouth.

"Naw, she just came by askin' about you Cuz," he shook his head. "I did think I had action, but naw, she wasn't wit it fam."

"Oh, okay, anybody else?"

Them nigga's laughed so loud that I began to feel some type of way.

"Next test," Amon began. "If you wanna fuck with a nigga, go over there to that bitch Wanda and knock the hell out that ho'. You know that big titty trick that been makin' the block hot?"

Now Wanda was a big bitch. She was nearly six feet and weighed well over two hundred pounds. With me being only five feet five inches, I had to be quick on my feet. My ass had to definitely 'bob and weave'.

"Where she at?" I questioned with my hand on my hip as I popped my gum.

Amon pointed down the street by the corner market. I looked down there and saw that she was standing by herself talking on her cell phone.

"Aight, I'll be right back," I assured as I turned away and drew some courage from deep within.

I plotted the whole way over there. I would have to catch her off guard to gain an advantage, so I decided to slap her first. Then I knew I had to hit her low and hard to take her down if need be.

Stepping up to her while she had her back turned, I tapped her shoulder to get her attention.

"What the fuck this lil' girl want," Wanda huffed to the person she was on the phone with. "Motherfucka's are bold around this camp!"

"Whack!" I reached back with an open hand and connected with Wanda's open cheek.

That bitch dropped her cell and began coming at me. I took a sideways stance and kicked that big ho' right in her knee. When she went down she turned her head upwards to talk shit.

"Whack!" I laced my fingers and used my combined fists to swing down at her.

The mighty blow I struck even surprised me. Blood splattered and I continued to hit her until she was completely helpless.

Thinking I was done with my mission, I glanced up at Amon to read him. He was wearing a smile while motioning me to come to him. I rushed right over to him with my heart racing as I attempted to regulate my breathing.

"Go on and get out of here before the law come," he laughed as he kissed my cheek. "You got heart and I like that. Meet me at my spot on the West Side around midnight so we can continue this little testing shit. You got a nigga intrigued wit' ya ass already."

Amon smacked my ass and shooed me away. I hurried and took my tail to my own side of town and got myself together for my next encounter with my new friend. First, I had to stop by my homegirl La'Karata's house. I needed to blow one after that shit.

"Bitch you won't believe what just happened over on the block Amon runs!" I shouted as soon as I stepped up in her living room.

"Hush, I just put lil' Ronnie down for a nap. You wake his ass up you gonna take him with you!" La'Karata warned. "I wish my sister hurry up and come get his bad ass!"

I took heed and began to whisper. I told her everything starting with me stepping to Amon and ending by telling her about my incident with Wanda. I had her ass cracking up.

"I know you lyin'!" she hollered then covered her mouth to whisper. "That ho' gon' get you girl!"

"Naw, I think she know now," I grinned.

"So you think you a bad bitch now?" La'Karata teased.

"Naw, you know fighting aint my thing. I'm just trying to get into Amon's pants and pockets," I admitted truthfully. "With that nigga's status, aint nobody gonna touch me."

My friend looked at me to see if I was serious.

"Yes bitch," I blurted out as if I could read her mind. "I'm fuckin' him while I'm getting' paid. Now what?"

Okay, yes, I was feeling myself but I knew Amon wanted a bold female, not a little weak ass bitch. If what I did that day didn't impress him, I didn't know what would…

Amon Rivers

I had to admit, lil mama had balls. I knew that none of the females in the hood had heart to step to Wanda's big ass. Wanda used that to her advantage and always punked them if she thought they were gonna try something with her.

When I told Ty to go smack her ass I thought she would punk out but she surprised me. She slapped fire from her ass. Not only did she slap big ass Wanda but she ended up boxing her out in front of the corner store.

I had to snatch lil mama up real quick and told her to get out of there. Last thing I needed was for her little feisty ass to get locked up. I sent her on her way with plans to meet up with her later. If lil mama played her cards right then she just might be able to be my girl.

I hollered at my boys for a quick minute before I decided to roll out.

"Ya know what's funny? When I first wanted to do this shit I was 13 years old and niggas laughed at me. Many folks thought I was joking and couldn't do any of the shit I said I could do. Now look..."

They listened closely as I put them up on game. I appreciated their attentiveness and it proved that they listened. When I finished I sat there and thought back to how things got started.

After DJ came up with the money for us to get on, I started shopping around. I needed to find out who had the best product. After I went through the elimination process there was only three dealers that had what I needed... Unfortunately Marco was one of them. He was immediately ruled out because of the heat he had on his ass.

My only other options were Twan and Whoop. From what I found out about both of them, they seemed on top of their shit. I requested to sit down with both of them and for a while they laughed me off. One of them asked why they should consider fucking with me.

None of that deterred me from my goal though. I knew between one or the both of them that I was going to come up real big. They could either hear me out and get on board or get crushed on my come up. Since Twan was a little younger than Whoop, he was the first one to come around.

Twan sent word through DJ that he would hear me out. I ain't gonna lie, I was nervous as fuck going into the meeting being that I was still a kid but I didn't let it show. I met up with Twan at one of his spots and told him what I had planned.

He heard me out not saying one word while I presented myself to him. Once I was done speaking he sat at the table with his hands folded and his fingers pressed to his lips. He looked at me coldly for a few moments before speaking.

"So what you're telling me is that if I change up the way I handle my operation and move a few people around I can capitalize a lot better?"

"That's exactly what I'm saying."

"So how do you propose that we do this thing kid? I see you got all ya ducks in a row and I'd be lying if I said that your plan wasn't genius cuz it is. Let's do this shit."

I was happy as fuck on the inside but I didn't let that shit show on the outside. I shook hands with Twan and let him know that DJ would be by to see him in the next couple of days. It was time to handle business.

I finished up my little spill to the fellas and took my ass home. I was still thinking about how I got to where I was. I had been up to a lot in the past few years.

That shit just flew by and before I knew it, I was already a millionaire. Can you believe that shit? At sixteen years old, I already was sitting on a good three million.

I invested my money and used off shore accounts for my shit. There was no way in hell that I was going to get caught the way some dumb ass dealers did.

I made sure my mom's was straight too. I'd grown tired of her working twelve hour shifts just to pay bills so once I got on I started taking care of her. I would give her money every week and because she had a legit job, she never was hassled about her deposits she made every week to her bank account.

After a year or so, my mom's had "saved" up enough money to buy a house. I was all for it and happy for her to move out the hood.

She no longer needed to live where I did my dirt. I went with her when she went house shopping and she bought a nice little house out in Lagrange. It was nice and way out the way from where I handled business.

I finished strolling down memory lane as I heard a knock at the door. I stayed in an old house on Sawyer Avenue right off Kedzie Avenue on the west side. It was located a few blocks from Humboldt Park where I hustled. Nobody knew about this house except Twan but we never did business there, only meetings between him and me.

I readied myself for lil mama because I knew she was ready for whatever. I opened the door and there she was looking as beautiful as ever. I let her in and we sat down with a drink. I wanted to get to know her so if I decided to take it to another level, I knew her inside and out.

Strangely enough, me and lil mama vibed on a totally different level. She was a lot smarter than I gave her credit for. She had a good head on her shoulders and could keep up with the conversation. I was impressed. I didn't think that a chick around my age could stimulate me in any way. I was proven wrong.

Ty'Keisha definitely had me intrigued. She kept up with every single thing I shot at her. Lil mama's game was tight and I was ready to make her mine. I waited a few weeks to let her know that I wanted her like she wanted me. She threw mad hints at my house that she was ready but I had to be sure. I definitely didn't want to rush into anything that I was going to regret at a later date. That shit just wasn't worth it.

The night finally came that I made an honest woman of Ty. We had agreed to meet up at the spot where we normally meet on Sawyer Avenue. I had a big night planned for us.

First, I was going to take her out to Michael Jordan's Steakhouse in downtown Chicago. Then we would be on our way to the Waldorf-Astoria Hotel, also in downtown Chicago, to get our grown up on. I wanted to make sure this was a night to remember for the both of us.

When we walked into our room at the Waldorf-Astoria, Ty's mouth dropped open. Being that I was underage, I had to get DJ to get the room for me. I had to make sure that I thanked his ass later because tonight was going to be a night to remember.

Ty'Keisha

Damn, that nigga made me go through hell and high water to get him to accept me as his girl. The shit he had me doing was crazy.

It was all good during the summer, but now that school was about to start I knew that I had to buckle down if I wanted to graduate. Amon was already finished with his education so his only commitment was to the streets.

"Dang baby, are you gonna miss me?"

"Where ya going?" Amon questioned sarcastically.

"School silly," I laughed as I playfully punched him in his arm. "Seriously, are you gonna miss me?"

"I doubt it," he shrugged and answered honestly. He was one cold motherfucker. "My ass stay busy baby, you know that."

"Well damn!"

"What?" he laughed and held me close to him to nibble on my ear.

"That wasn't the answer I was looking for," I answered truthfully.

"Can we just enjoy our time together? We're staying in this fly ass hotel, ordering room service and I'm dickin' you down whenever you want. Now, you still complaining baby?"

Amon was right. I was being a little spoiled brat and I knew he didn't like that shit.

"Baby," I spoke as his cell rang. I wanted to grab his attention so I fondled his manhood.

Do you know that this nigga had the nerve to push me up off him to answer the motherfucker? Ooooo, I was heated.

I was so irritated that I didn't even want to ear hustle, but when I heard La'Karata's name my ears stood straight up.

"What she want with me and she know good and damn well I'm with Ty?" Amon whispered when he saw me coming towards the bathroom.

Amon held up his finger and closed the door on me. I had to take a deep breath before I went in on the fool. If it had something to do with La'Karata, it involved me too. Hell that was supposed to be my homegirl, my ace boon coon...

"Tell her to meet me at the spot in an hour," I heard Amon say in a low tone before disconnecting his call.

Taking his time in the bathroom, Amon came out smelling fresh and looking damn good. I didn't dare ask him about his phone conversation. I had a better idea.

"Where you going baby?" I inquired as I drew him near enough to steal a kiss.

"I just gotta go check the trap real quick baby," he smiled as he held me and looked in my eyes. "I'll be back in two hours top. Why don't you order up some strawberries and whip cream so we can see what that's all about."

"Oh, you tasting me tonight boo?"

"Hell yeah," he smiled as he smothered me with kisses. "All that bomb ass head that you be throwing on me on the daily, shit, that's the least I can do."

"Oh shit," I thought to myself as I released Amon so that he could leave.

"Call me if you need me Ty," he suggested before walking out.

My ass hurried the hell up and showered and got dressed. I dialed a taxi while I did my hair up in a bun. By the time I got down to the lobby, my ride was out front waiting.

I hopped in the cab and had the driver take me directly to Amon's spot on the West Side. When I arrived, I spotted La'Karata's car right away.

Instead of rushing the situation, I sat back and watched the way they interacted.

"Oh hell naw," I gasped as I saw my homegirl pushing up on Amon.

Still, I made no move. I just sat there and continued to peep the situation. I even cracked the window so that I could try to hear what they were saying.

"So what's up?" La'Karata flirted with her hands on her hips.

"Yo, what is it that you want with me?" Amon asked suspiciously. "Y'all tryna set me up and shit?"

"No, I promise not to tell Ty," La'Karata begged. "It's just that I want to see for myself what she's always bragging on."

That bitch had the audacity to grab my man's dick. That did it!

I must have hopped my ass out of the taxi so fast that I almost fell and lost my balance. That gave me time enough to focus on the matter at hand instead of flying off the handle.

"What's up with you touching my man like that yo?" I questioned La'Karata as I approached them.

Amon stood back and let me handle things.

"What?"

"What my ass bitch," I smirked.

"Bitch?"

"Yeah bitch!" I yelled as I swung on her.

The fight was over before it began. I really didn't want to do it, but it was a matter of respect. I didn't play that shit.

"I swear you better not eva talk to me again Ty!" La'Karata screamed while picking up her loose pieces of her weave that I had snatched out. "I see you wanna show ya ass, but I know all ya little secrets and I can't wait to bust ya ass up."

"Huh?" Amon questioned as he stepped to La'Karata. "If you have to say something, say the shit right here and now. That is if you are the bold bitch ya claim to be ma."

"Oh, I got ya digits," she huffed as she hurried to her car. "Trust and believe this shit ain't over!"

Soon as the chick skeeted off, Amon started to interrogate me. I knew that shit was coming, but I didn't have shit to hide. I had been totally faithful to him the entire time we had been dating, so whatever La'Karata was talking about was a damn lie.

"Baby," I began. "Let that bitch tell you whatever she wants. She ain't doing shit but selling wolf tickets and I'm sure I can discredit each and every accusation that the trick dishes out. Believe that shit baby."

"I believe you baby," Amon laughed as he hugged me then shooed me off. "And don't be following a nigga around either."

"Whatever, wit' ya old sneaky ass!" I smirked. "Just meet me back at the room. You remember what you promised me when you got back right?"

"Yes baby," he smiled and kissed me. "Have it ready for me aight?"

"Gotcha baby," I giggled as I went and hopped in the waiting taxi.

I waved and blew my man a kiss and I sat back and contemplated on how to handle La'Karata. That bitch had another ass whooping coming, with her name written all over the shit...

Amon Rivers

Man shorty was buggin'! I didn't want to have shit to do with her ratchet ass homegirl but just had to find out what she wanted with me. You never could trust those ho's, so it was better to be safe than sorry. Last thing I expected was for her to come at me like she did and Lord knows I definitely didn't expect Ty to follow a nigga neither.

When ol' girl went to grabbing on my dick and shit all I wanted to do was knock her ass out. I couldn't stand bitches like her. She was lucky that I wasn't a grimey ass dude. When I was with a chick then that was who I was with. I couldn't get down with hopping from chick to chick nor could I get down with a chick that smashed any of my homies.

I couldn't help but laugh though. Shit was funny when Ty went at her ass. I couldn't do shit but stand back and let baby girl handle her business. One thing I learned about her already was that she could definitely hold her own. I let her do her thing before I checked her ass about following me. Last thing I needed was my girl making my trap hot so after all the commotion died down I sent her on her way. I had business to take care of and I didn't need her to know nothing about it.

I walked into the trap to meet Twan. We were implementing the next phase of our plan. We got rid of all the weak links in his operation. I made sure to do extensive checks on anybody who he felt was an essential part of his team. I needed to know who was who and what issues they had. We didn't need anybody who could jeopardize what we were about to do.

I have to admit that Twan was on top of his shit. His top lieutenants were as thorough as they come. They were from the streets and lived the streets. None of them ever had been arrested either which was pretty impressive. That was another reason that made me really want to fuck with Twan.

After we went through his lieutenants then it was on to his workers in the trap. A few had to be let go but they got a severance package for their cooperation. I know what you're thinking. Why in the fuck am I talking about severance packages like this is a real company or some shit right? Well that's because it was.

All positions, with the exception of those of us at the top, had an opportunity for advancement. I wanted to offer our workers the same thing a regular nine-to-five gig did except without the taxes. Everybody had a weekly paycheck that was determined by how many hours they trapped.

Everybody who ran a trap had to keep track of their workers and their worker's hours. It was their job to make sure their workers were paid as well. As long as the money was right and the workers always came straight up, all was good. This was just one of my ideas that I relayed to Twan.

Another idea was that besides trapping, we required all of our workers to have another source of income so they were encouraged to go to school. We didn't need a team of dumb ass niggas to work with. Dumb niggas made dumb decisions and we couldn't have that.

We actually had quite a few smart dudes on our team so I took advantage of my genius status to help them get where they needed to be. I helped with schoolwork, taught classes and tutored whoever needed help. If we were going to run a company then we all had to think alike.

By the time the meeting was over and I had strategized with Twan over a few more things, we were all set. All we had to do now was set up the next meeting with the connect and we were all systems go. Now that I was finished handling business it was time to go handle baby girl. I couldn't wait to get all up in that again.

I made it back to the hotel after being gone most of the day to find shorty sleeping. I quickly took a shower so I could join her in bed. I promised her that I was going to taste her that night and I always kept my word.

I pulled the blanket back and noticed that she was naked as the day she was born. Her skin was smooth and her pussy was shaven clean. I observed her lips that were glistening with her juices. I couldn't wait to discover the taste of it.

I placed light kisses up her legs as I spread them open. She mumbled incoherently, but didn't wake up. That was the green light I was looking for.

Taking my time, I made my way up to her treasure box. It looked so scrumptious. Damn! I got myself excited until I couldn't take it anymore then dove in headfirst.

Baby girl's shit was sweet and tasting her was the best thing of my young life. Or so I thought at the time...

While swirling my tongue around in her love pot, I felt her stir. Ty reached her hands out to touch the top of my head and rubbed it. That shit did nothing but make me go harder.

As she began to twirl her hips, I gripped them and help guide her in a steady motion. Meanwhile, I stiffened my tongue and let her fuck my face while I held on to her hips.

When I felt her legs start to clamp together, I held my head in place to ensure a proper orgasm. Trust and believe, I was aiming to please and it didn't take long...

The second I felt a warm, sweet liquid shoot out, I lapped it all up. Apparently, Ty wasn't quite finished because her hips continued to twirl. That was my cue to keep it going even after she screamed out for me to stop.

Next thing I knew, I was bringing her ass to yet another orgasm. I never had a chick who squirted before but then again, I hadn't been with a lot of females. I was very meticulous about who I fucked with on an intimate level.

Ty was only the third chick I had been with since I started having sex so I was still learning as I went. I didn't tell anybody that though because that was my business.

"Come on baby," Ty pleaded with her eyes. "I want you... No, no... I need you."

Obliging, I climbed in between Ty's shaking legs and rubbed the tip of my dick up and down her gooey center. She shivered again as I slowly slid inside of her. Shorty was tight as fuck! She was definitely worth keeping and I didn't even bother to strap up as I dove inside of her like I usually did.

I just hoped and prayed that I wouldn't live to regret that moment...

Ty'Keisha

"He went up in you raw?" My stepsister Marda gasped in disbelief as we chopped it up at the diner down the street. "Don't he know you aint on birth control?"

"No, not exactly and besides, we've been kicking it since before my senior year." I laughed and played it off. "Anyway, what would be so bad about having a kid by...?"

"By who, another kid?" she clowned. "Now that you graduated this year, you need to consider going to college."

"Well he's banked up like a man!" I defended as I rubbed my belly. "What I need to go to college for? Shit, my man is gonna take care of me for the rest of my life! Believe that shit!"

I imagined what it would be like to be pregnant. "I can still finish school." I thought

"Look, you let that nigga fuck ya head all the way up boo," my girl clowned. "I aint got shit else to say."

I let it die because I knew that she was absolutely right. My mind was on nothing but money and the status of the streets. Amon had both...

"Let me get up out of here," Marda pouted in disappointment. "You really need to get your priorities in check Sis. I can see you doing so much more than just fuckin' with a street hustla. Why don't you just think about that?"

Ignoring my stepsister totally, I twisted my nose up and slid my nearly full plate away from me. I wanted so badly to tell her to but the hell out, but I had too much respect for her.

I had to admit, Marda was the only positive person in my life that I could look up to. Our father was a drug dealer that neither of us spoke to and my mother was a closet smoker. Both my aunts on both sides were crackheads and our dad's brother was on heroin. What a fucking family...

"Call me later," she waved before pulling off.

Knowing good and damn well her ass had an attitude she smiled right through that shit and kept it pushing. Hell, I wasn't mad at her. I could only do her in hour intervals once a year anyways. If it was more than that we would be at one another's throat.

Hopping in my ride, I headed to the spot to do a drive by. My nosey ass couldn't help it. As fine and powerful as Amon was, I just knew his ass was honey dipping on the side. A bitch like me wasn't having it. If I had to whoop every female in the state of Illinois to keep them at arm's length when it came to Amon, I would.

"Damn," I shouted as I rolled by Amon's main spot. I peeped his car right away.

That niggas windows were tinted, but the light from his cell phone lit up the inside of the car just enough for me to see that he was in there. Thing was, he wasn't alone.

Okay, I was in a position that I could either check his ass at home, or go over there and check the situation right then. While deciding, I flipped a bitch at the corner and parked on the other side of the street. I hit the engine and turned off the lights. Just as I was getting out of my car, so was him and the chick.

"Call me later boo," she smiled, rubbed his chest and blew a kiss before walking towards her ride across the street.

Rushing back to my car, I started it up and drove down the street. I caught the bitch as soon as she stepped her ass off the curb.

"What the fuck?" I heard Amon yell as I nicked the chick just enough to send her flying into the grass by her whip.

Instead of stopping, I just kept going. I knew that nigga was about to call me. It was his move.

"Ring"

Damn, that was fast. I didn't have enough to think shit out, so I let his first three calls go to voicemail. I answered on the fourth.

"Are you fucking crazy?" Amon hollered out. "That was my connect baby! Why did you do that shit?"

My nerves were wrecked. I knew right then and there I had fucked up. I didn't have shit to say so I hit the disconnect button and powered off my phone.

"Why am I so jealous?" I questioned myself. "Marda was right. I need to get my shit together."

Going straight to my mother's house, I parked around the side and ran inside to lock myself in my room. I knew that Amon wouldn't come over there clowning. At least I hoped.

Man, I wasn't in my room a good fifteen minutes before I heard the doorbell ring. A familiar voice came next.

"Oh, how wrong I was."

I must have damn near broke my damn neck trying to get in the living room before Amon busted me up about hitting his little friend. Honestly I didn't give a fuck who the bitch was; she shouldn't have been flirting with my man like that. Once she touched him that was it.

Stopping dead in my tracks, I locked eyes with Amon. The anger in them said it all. Funny thing was, he straightened his expression before addressing my mother.

"Excuse me moms," he began. "Can I please talk to Ty in private?"

"Why the hell you askin' me?" she snapped as she took her ass right back to her room. "You need to be askin' the person you want to see. That seems to make more damn sense. Didn't you say you graduated early and had a high IQ or some shit? Hell, you don't seem so bright to me."

My mother smirked with the few teeth she had left in her mouth and got to moving. She was so fucking embarrassing...

Amon Rivers

I was not in the mood for Ty's mom's smartass mouth so I let her comment slide. What I was focused on was the fact that Ty pulled the shit that she pulled. No I didn't tell her my connect was a woman but that was none of her damn business. The less she knew the better.

I snatched her up by her arm after I was sure that her mom's was back in her own room with the door shut.

"What the fuck I tell yo lil jealous about shit like that Ty?"

"I know baby but I can't help it. I don't like other women looking at you let alone touching you boo. I'm sorry."

"Man sorry ain't gonna cut it this time. You know how much ass ima have to kiss to keep Milagros as my connect? That shit ain't gonna be easy. Ima leave ya ass here for a few days while you figure out what the fuck ya problem is."

"A few days? But baby wait. If you need me to I'll apologize to ol girl and everything, I will. She should understand where I'm coming from woman to woman."

"Nah the only thing she understands is money. The fact that I make her a lot of that might be what saves my ass with her. With you, I don't know though. I might have to just be cool on you for a while."

I didn't care what else lil mama had to say because I was done talking. I walked out the room and towards the front door as I heard her crying and screaming my name. I could give two fucks about her feelings right then because she was starting to fuck with my money. There was no way I was about to let that happen.

I hopped back into my whip and called Milagros. Boy did I hate having to clean shit up but that one was on account of me. It was my fault that I had a jealous ass, stalking ass girlfriend who couldn't understand to play her position. That was part of the reason I didn't want a girl in the first place but I just couldn't help myself. The chick had me intrigued.

I waited patiently as I heard the phone ring on the other side and hoped that Ty hadn't fucked up my deal with Milagros.

"Ya know Amon, I didn't peg you for the drama type. What the fuck was that earlier?"

"Milagros I'm really sorry about that. Nobody is to blame about that but me. I am hoping though that this doesn't stop us from working together."

"No it doesn't because you make me a ton of money on a regular basis. However, if that shit happens again, whoever she is, will be a dead woman walking. Do I make myself clear?"

"I understand completely Milagros. Thank you."

"No thank you Amon. Ya know, if you weren't so fucking young I woulda made you mine. You have the heart of a boss, the mind of a CEO and the iron fist of a dictator. Those are all the great things needed when becoming a Kingpin and you're well on the way."

"Well Milagros I'm flattered and if that offer is still on the table in a few years I might take you up on that."

"It will be Amon. Goodbye."

With that she hung up. That thought alone left me with some serious decisions to make. Milagros basically told me that she'd groom me for greatness. With her as my business partner and lover, we could take over the world... literally. I shot a quick text to Ty and let her know that the little stunt she pulled wasn't cool and I didn't need those few days to think some shit through. We were done.

After I did that I cut my phone off because I just knew that once she got that text she was going to start blowing up my phone wanting answers. I didn't have time for the drama no more and I hadn't even been kicking it with lil mama that long. Nah I was on to bigger and better things. The first thing being was the money I was making hand over fist. Pretty soon I was gonna be a king.

The King of Chicago. Yeah, I liked the sound of that...

Ty'Keisha

When Amon went storming out of my place, I knew that nigga was .45 hot. He had to have been to tell me he was done. I couldn't let him go that easily. I had to come up with a plan.

"Damn, I always fuck up a good thing with my jealous behavior!" I fussed silently as I paced back and forth across my bedroom carpet.

Taking a seat in my swivel desk chair, I eased my toes in and out of my plush pink house shoes. The softness relaxed me and when I closed my eyes it all came to me.

"I'm gonna tell him I'm pregnant!"

I knew Amon was the type of man that would take care of his seed at all costs. He would protect me and give me whatever I wanted. That's exactly what I was going to do. If I could ever get his ass to answer the phone...

In the meantime, I called my homegirl Sherry that lived in the same complex as I did. I knew she would help me if the price was right.

"You want what?" she laughed at my request for a sample of her piss.

"Yes, I have a sterile cup from the doctor's office. I will bring it to you." I explained.

"What ya gonna do for me Ty?"

"I got fifty for you and a blunt of some good," I teased knowing that what I was offering was way more than she was expecting.

"Shit, ya ass aint up here yet?" he giggled. "I need those ends."

"This is just between me and you," I reminded. If you keep ya trap shut then I may have a little more for you next week."

"My fuckin' lips are sealed!" she promised. "A bitch knows when not to fuck up a good thing."

I laughed and rushed my ass straight up to her apartment. I got what I needed and took my ass home and powered on my computer along with the printer.

Traveling directly to Google, I searched the web for positive pregnancy test templates. I needed a legitimate document to back up my positive pregnancy test stick that I was going to provide as well. I had to make sure I was able to answer any question he may have had.

When I was ready, I dressed in a hoody and sweats and went to find Amon. He had to listen to me, especially when I allowed the tears to flow. That would be the easy part, because my ass was hurt behind losing a gold mine like him. I needed him and I was willing to get him, by any means necessary…

"Ty, seriously?" Amon smirked as he met me halfway up the block.

I could tell that he didn't want to make a scene in front of his boys and I totally understood that. I was coming in peace and I needed him to know that.

"I'm sorry," I sniffled. "I've just been a little emotional lately."

"Why's that Ty?" he questioned suspiciously.

Slowly retrieving the stick and paper out of my pocket, I showed him. His reaction was quick.

"So what ya sayin' shorty?"

"Don't that say it all?"

Snatching me by the hand, he dragged me to the store at the corner and bought another pregnancy test. Amon then handed it to me and guided me to the bathroom in the back.

"Y'all aight?" the store clerk clowned. "Let me know how that shit works out. I got a cigar up here for you if need be Amon!"

"Whatever," he waved him off and handed me the package. "I'll be right here when you come out too."

"Damn, you don't trust me baby?" I cried trying to lay it on as thick as possible.

"Are you gonna take the test or do I have to take you up the street to the clinic and make a damn scene Ty?"

"I'm going!" I huffed as I opened the bathroom door and went in, locking it behind me.

Yes, I was a smart motherfucker. I brought the rest of the piss that Sherry gave me. I had that shit right in my pocket.

Using only a few drops, I dripped it across the streamline and waited. While I did so, I flushed the toiled and washed my hands.

"Knock-knock"

"What?"

"Come out, I wanna see."

As I opened the door, the two lines slowly appeared.

"Damn, I guess you wasn't lyin'." He sighed in amazement. "We gonna have to talk about this shit later. Thanks to you I have to work a lil harder these next couple of days to get shit right."

"So when will I see you baby?" I whined as I tried my best to hold in my smile.

"I'll be by around 11 or 12," he promised as he kissed me on the forehead. "Now take ya ass home and stay out of these fuckin' streets ma'."

Damn, I wanted to skip my ass up out of that store whistling and grinning, but I knew better. Instead I kept up my charade.

"Baby, can you get me a cold drink and some chips please?"

"Get what you want up out of here and I'll call to see what else you need before I come, aight?" he smiled.

Hurrying to get my little snacks, I thanked Amon and took my ass home to wait on my man. I knew I had to have my story straight, so I had some rehearsing to do...

Amon Rivers

One minute I was entertaining the thought of Milagros and her offer. The next minute, things changed. When Ty came on the block and handed me the pregnancy test and paper I knew shit got real. I made her ass take an extra test just in case. You know how bitches can get especially when a nigga got bank.

When she took that second test and it came back positive I knew what I had to do. Milagros's offer had to jump on the back burner because I was about to be a daddy.

Now let's make no mistake about things. I was about to take her up on her offer for sure but first I had to make sure my baby mama was straight. Even though I was only seventeen years old, I still had a responsibility to take care of. Seeing as I didn't have my father, I was gonna make sure my seed had me at his or her beck and call.

First thing was first though. There was money to be made so I had to handle some shit on the streets.

After hitting all the traps, counting and re-counting the money and checking in with Twan, I placed a call to Ty. I wanted to know if she needed anything and because she was pregnant I was planning on running all up in that gushy thing.

Ty asked for some Sabor Latino and said it didn't matter what I got. I drove down North Avenue towards the restaurant to grab her some food. I ordered something for myself as well when I got there.

Once I had our food I jumped back in my whip and made my way to Ty's spot. I parked, grabbed the grub and hopped out. I didn't even make it to the door before her ass had it open with a big, stupid ass grin on it.

Soon as she saw the bag of food, her eyes lit up. Before I knew it, she had snatched the sack from me just as I turned around to close and lock the door.

"Awww bae you got my favorite."

"Girl you know I couldn't come in here without that Carne Asada plate. You woulda kicked my ass."

"Well at least you know."

We laughed as we made small talk about the baby. At first when she told me I was in shock. After I let it sink in I was actually starting to get excited about things. I knew my seed wasn't gonna want for shit. I wanted to see where Ty's head was at so I decided to pick her brain.

"So since we got a baby coming I was thinking of getting you your own crib. What you think?"

"Really?"

"Yes really. I can't have y'all living with ya moms and shit. You don' graduated and grown. I think it's time. Besides, my baby is gonna need his or her own space."

"Ohemgee! I can't wait! When can I start looking?"

"You can start tomorrow shorty. Just let me know when you find something that you like and let me know how much it is. I got you."

Ty jumped in my lap almost spilling her food. She started placing kisses all over my face and neck. That shit right there had a nigga horny right off the back. It had my man standing at attention and damn near poking out my fucking pants.

Without breaking our kissing when I stood up, I held her tightly as she wrapped her legs around my waist. Holding her securely, I walked up the stairs to her room carrying her small frame. I kicked the door closed behind us and only removed my hand from her ass long enough to lock the door. Lying Ty down on the bed, I started removing her clothes. Not wanting to, I had to break our kiss so I could take her shirt off. She eagerly took mine off right before her hands flew to my pants.

She unbuckled, unsnapped and unzipped my pants so fast that I didn't even know she had my dick out until I felt her mouth on it. Throwing my head back in ecstasy as she took me in, I felt my dick hit the back of her throat. Damn, baby girl was really bringing her A-game that night.

The shit that had me tripping was when Ty kept slurping and slobbing like her life depended on it. It had a niggas toes curling and shit. Before I could object, I felt myself getting ready to cum so I tried to pull her off me. She pushed my hands away and kept going while she did this suction thing with her mouth. That was it...

I let off in her mouth. She gagged, but she didn't spit it out. Even though that shit turned me on, that shit couldn't be good for my baby. I would nip that shit in the bud later though. Right then I was about to tear her little ass up.

As she pulled off the rest of her clothes, I stepped out my jeans so I could finish what we started. First, I heaved her body to the edge of the bed and plowed into her wet pussy. She yelped out in pain upon entrance then got into the rhythm that I had going on. She was throwing it at me and I was catching everything. When it got to be too much, I pulled out and told her to turn over. Obliging, Ty tooted her big booty up at me and I smacked it.

"Hell yeah"

She squealed in delight as I entered her again. I gripped her hips and started stroking her fast. I felt her pussy muscles clench up on me so I knew she was about to cum. Even though two tests said she was pregnant, I wasn't taking any chances.

Just as I was busting my nut I pulled out of Ty and shot my load on her back. Realizing what I did, she hopped up mad as hell.

"What the fuck you do that for Amon?"

"Oh I'm Amon now? A few minutes ago I was bae."

"Yeah so. You acting like I'm some thot or something by pulling out and skeeting on my damn back. I'm already pregnant so it ain't like you can get me pregnant again."

"So. I felt like pulling out. What you mad for?"

Ty didn't say shit else to me. She just huffed and puffed as she went into the bathroom slamming the door. If this was any indication of what her attitude was going to be like while she was pregnant then I was going to stay as far away from her as possible. Last thing I needed was to deal with an overly emotional pregnant broad.

I quickly dressed before I headed out. I was going to tell Ty that I was leaving but when I went to the bathroom door, I found it locked. I put my ear to the door and heard her loud sobs.

I started to feel bad, but then again I didn't. If she was on some bullshit then I'd find out soon enough.

It was time to hit the streets again. There was always money to be made and if I wanted to retire by the time I was thirty then I had to stay on my grind.

Leaving Ty's house, I hopped in my whip and made my way to the block. I felt like pulling an all-nighter so these cats knew I wasn't above getting my hands dirty. Pretty soon all I'd have to do was give a demand and niggas would jump at my word. In another year I planned to have the city on lockdown. It was my time to shine...

Ty'Keisha

On my way home from meeting with Amon, I stopped by the pharmacy and purchased a couple of ovulation kits. My homegirl had told me that it was the best way to find out when I could get pregnant.

Ripping open the box as soon as I got into my room, I followed the directions.

"Shit, I better get myself together!" I yelled as I showered and got ready for Amon to come over.

The test said it was a high chance for me to become pregnant if I had sex within twenty-four to thirty-six hours. I had to do what I had to do, but shit didn't turn out the way that I expected. I did everything I had planned, but that shit seemed to backfire.

"I can't believe that nigga just did his duty on my back like that!" I complained as I jumped in the shower to clean off. That's when I noticed the sticky substance dripping out of my stash.

"Obviously he didn't pull out as quick as he thought!" I laughed. "I wonder why he did that shit."

The only reason could have been was that he didn't believe me. I had to be a little smarter...

Rushing over to my desk, I pulled up the proof of pregnancy document I had created on my computer. I switched the date of the doctor visit and printed out two copies. After folding it up with two creases, I slid it into a legal sized envelope that I had already made with the doctor's office logo. It looked way more legit than the last one Amon just crumbled up and threw away.

"Bam," I smiled feeling proud of my deception. "Bet he think twice next time."

That was my insurance just in case I didn't get pregnant that last time. I couldn't wait until the last minute and not be prepared... I had to stay ready!

****

It took me until the next day to get Amon to come over and when he did, he claimed he was dead tired. He was giving me every indication that he didn't believe that I was pregnant. That was when I felt as if I had no choice but to give him the letter. When I did, he had the fucking audacity to act as if he didn't need it for confirmation. He claimed to have believed me in the first place.

Oh, he was a lying motherfucker. That's just why he shoved that shit in his jacket pocket as soon as he thought I wasn't looking.

"I gotta go baby," Amon informed me as he kissed my lips and got up to leave. "Oh, and have you been looking for a place?"

"Yeah, I found a few spots," I lied trying to buy some time. "We can go look at them this weekend."

"Aight, hook that shit up and call me later," he smiled as he closed the door behind him.

"Fuck that!" I screamed feeling frustrated that I couldn't get him to give me the business.

The window for me being able to conceive was about to close and I couldn't let that shit happen. I had to do the unthinkable and call my old faithful fuck buddy Aiden. That nigga was always available and I knew that he wasn't sleeping with no one else. He was a momma's boy that went to the Catholic High School on the other side of town. Good thing was, he favored Amon a whole lot.

Dialing him up, I got my spill together.

"Hey Aiden, I really need to see you right now," I begged as if I was in dire need.

"I have a meeting in an hour," he replied sounding torn.

"Please, I won't keep you that long."

Aiden quickly agreed and was outside my house within twenty minutes. My mother was all up in my look so I met him at his car and jumped in.

"What's up Ty?"

"Can we just drive?" I pouted as I fixed my dress enough to hide that I wasn't wearing any panties.

"Yeah, anywhere particular?"

"Go up the old road on the east side where we used to go park and talk. I feel more comfortable there." I persuaded with a rub to his thigh.

Along the ride he began talking about taking up ministry. It was totally throwing my vibe off. I needed one thing from him at the moment and talking about Jesus wasn't one of them.

"I miss you," I whispered as I fondled him though his gym shorts.

His dick jumped to attention and as soon as it did, I released it and began to get an oral hold on it. Now before that, I had never gone down on Aiden, but I was willing to do what it took to ensure some unprotected sex. That was going to be another hurdle...

"Ty, are you sure..." he gasped as I deep throated him a couple of times.

We were just arriving at the spot when I felt the veins in his dick pulsating. I knew that meant an ejaculation was near. I didn't want that just yet.

As he placed his car in park, I straddled his lap and began bucking wildly before he could object.

"Oh my..." Aiden yelled out as he gripped my hips and released a load up in me.

Instead of hopping up, I stayed in that position as long as possible. I kissed his mouth so he couldn't speak.

"Wait, wait..." he blurted out the second I let him up for air. "We didn't use..."

"It's okay Aiden," I assured him and added a fib. "I'm on the pill and you're the only one I'm sleeping with."

Aiden sighed and held me tightly. "I love you Ty."

My heart melted. No one had ever told me those words before. Not even my mother...

I remained silent as I moved to the passenger seat and grabbed a napkin from his glove box to wipe off. I strapped in and looked at Aiden. "Love you too boo."

As I released those words, I actually seemed to mean them. Sad thing was, a relationship with him just wasn't in the cards...

Amon Rivers

This bitch was trying to be funny. Ok so maybe I was being a little paranoid after two pregnancy tests and a doctor's note, but I wasn't stupid. She didn't let tell me about this so-called doctor's visit until after the fact. How could she think that I wouldn't want to be a part of that? Not only that but shorty was acting real funny when I busted on her back the other day.

"If I find out that her ass ain't really pregnant ima fuck her up. For now, ima just chill."

I hit the block and made my rounds. Business was going good for me and Twan. We ran a tight ship and so far there were no glitches. While we were growing larger in numbers, other crews were dwindling away to nothing.

That chump ass dude Marco got bagged not too long after I hooked up with Twan. I bet his dumb ass wished he would have listened to me back then. I laughed at the thought.

Twan was a good businessman. He didn't let his ego or pride get in the way of making money. That's what I liked about him. Whenever I made a suggestion about something that could make us even more money, he was down for it.

Twan and I started discussing his exit from the game not that long ago. He said with me doing the numbers I was doing and making the moves that I made, I had set him up for life. He was pushing thirty years old and he was ready to retire. I had learned a lot from him. He told me that he was passing me the torch and with my eighteenth birthday approaching, he was going to make the announcement at my party.

I remember the conversation like it was yesterday and I'll never forget it.

"Amon, you've made me a lot of money in the last few years. I'll admit that I was skeptical at first when I found out that you wanted to sit down with me. I'm glad I did it though."

"Thanks man I really appreciate that. I didn't think you'd hear me out though."

"At first I wasn't because you were just a kid. I was wondering what a 13 year old could want with me but then I found out it was you. You're a legend in the making and don't even know it kid."

"Well I'm glad you took a chance on me. Now we both living good."

"Living good indeed. That's something I wanted to talk to you about young blood. I've had a good run and I wanna keep it that way so I'm out. You're the new king and I'll be announcing it at your birthday party."

"Word? For real yo I'm honored that you're passing me the torch. I ain't gotta worry about no static from anybody do I?"

"Nah kid. Everybody who's important knows and those who don't get with the program can get gone. That's my word."

"Bet that. I'm ready OG and I won't let you down."

"I know you won't Amon but always stay on point like you've been doing. We went from thousands being made to millions. Remember though, heavy is the head that wears the crown."

"Gotcha!

My eighteenth birthday was in less than a month. It was my time to shine and best believe that I was gonna do just that: SHINE! I rode out to North Riverside Mall on Harlem Avenue and Cermak Road to find me a fit. I had to be fresh as fuck when I stepped in the door. All I knew was that everybody was going to be in attendance and I was told to dress to impress. I don't know what Twan and Milagros had hooked up for my birthday but I knew it was gonna be killer.

I ran through the mall grabbing all the shit that caught my eye. I knew that with all the clothes I bought I'd definitely have something to wear. I made my way back to my car and tossed all my bags into the back seat. I had just pulled off and Big Pun's 100% was bumping through my speakers when my phone started to ring. I glanced down at the screen and noticed it was DJ calling me. I paid it no attention because I didn't feel like answering the phone. When DJ called back again I knew something was up. I lowered the music and answered the phone.

"Yo kid where you at?"

"I'm just leaving the mall. What's up though? Did something happen?"

"Yeah man it's bad. It's all bad. It's Twan yo."

"What about Twan? What happened Cuz?"

"I just need you to get to headquarters ASAP!"

"Say no more. I'm on my way."

I flew down Harlem Avenue and hit the 290. The normal 20-minute drive only took me ten minutes. I pulled up to headquarters and jumped out my whip leaving it running. Everybody knew my car so I wasn't worried about nobody touching my shit. When I walked in everybody stopped talking and stared at me. I looked around the room and noticed that a few people avoided eye contact with me but that was the least of my worries at the time.

"Somebody gonna tell me something or what?"

"Man Amon," DJ started.

"Yo just spit it the fuck out."

"OK man Twan was shot and killed earlier today. When he didn't show up for the meeting with me and Que, I knew something was up. I called Milagros and she sent someone to find out. She confirmed a little bit ago. That's when I called you."

"*What the fuck*? How could that shit happen? Anybody know about any beef anyone had against him?"

I slowly looked around the room and I noticed the same two niggas who wouldn't make eye contact with me were still avoiding me. I was gonna check behind them niggas but for now I had to get up with Milagros and get shit situated with Twan. Man I was going to miss my dawg.

PART TWO
THE MYTH

Ty'Keisha

Shit was fucked up. Yeah, I actually got pregnant, but my dates were off by weeks. Even though my period told me I was due on one date, my levels were determining something different. I was totally confused. It was getting harder and harder to keep up with all the lies that I had to constantly tell.

"Ty, I wanna come to your next doctor's appointment." Amon demanded as he stuffed his face with a fully loaded bacon cheeseburger. "Your stomach isn't even that big and you're almost six months!"

"I'm small, so I'm probably gonna have a small little girl," I guessed.

"When the fuck you have an ultrasound?" Amon spat as he stood up and approached me with an attitude. "You said you wasn't gonna get one! Didn't I tell you if you changed your mind I wanted to be there?"

I could tell that Amon had a major attitude. That was the angriest I had ever seen him. I didn't know how to answer him.

"Huh?"

"Huh?" he snapped. "Huh nothin'! You heard me now answer me! Why didn't you tell me you were having a fuckin' ultrasound? When did you get it? How long have you known we're having a daughter?"

"I didn't! I mean I don't know! I'm just guessing," I spoke truthfully.

Thank goodness, I was a quick thinker. He bought right into the shit. At least for a second or two...

"So what the hell are you hiding from me Ty!" he barked getting upset all over again. "That's why it's hard to trust ya ass! I need a girl that's a team player!"

Now that we had finally moved in together, it had become more difficult to hide shit. I wasn't even sure how far along I was or who the daddy was at that point. All I knew was since there was a great chance of it being Aiden's, I couldn't risk the chance of Amon finding out until I knew for sure myself.

"Fuck," I huffed as I watched Amon grab his keys and storm towards the door. "Where are you going?"

"On the block," he blasted as he stood in the doorway. "Don't wait up!"

"For real nigga?"

"For real!"

"So you aint gonna spend no time with me? I thought you were happy about us having this baby?" I whined and hoped that he would lighten up a bit and forgive me.

"You make it hard for me to get happy about shit that comes out of ya mouth Ty," Amon spoke honestly. "I gotta clear my head. I can't think up in here!"

Without allowing another begging word to escape my lips, Amon turned and slammed the door behind him. My heart dropped.

The tears came as soon as he left. I didn't have anyone to talk to but Aiden. I hadn't spoken to his ass in months. I thought it was best since I was starting to have feelings for him. That shit wouldn't do nothing but complicate things more, but I needed to talk to someone. He was my only choice...

Since he didn't have my cell number and I couldn't take the chance at him getting it, I blocked my call and dialed him. He answered right away as if he knew it was me.

"Hello?"

"Hey Aiden," I spoke softly.

"Ty'Keisha?" he yelled out. "Is that you?"

"Yeah, it's me," I sighed knowing that a million questions were about to come my way.

"Where have you been? Are you alright? What happened to your cell? Did you break it? Did you get a new number? Where are you?" Aiden interrogated in an excited tone.

"Whoa, shit," I yelled. "I'm okay. I just need time to myself occasionally, you know?"

"Yeah, I understand baby. All you have to do is just talk to me. Let me know what's going on and I got you," he promised with sincerity in his voice.

"I know Aiden," I acknowledged. "Sometimes you just have to find your own way and have your own back."

"Don't eva feel that way Ty'Keisha," he replied. "I'll always be here for you if you let me."

Damn, that was a good nigga. He was going to make some woman a hell of a husband, just not me. I was too focused on the big prize. I needed the money and all Aiden had was a regular job making regular salary driving a regular car. Hell, he was just a regular nigga…

"Where are you?" Aiden repeated sounding anxious. "Let me come to you. I need to see you Ty'Keisha."

I was starving and didn't have a way to get to get some food. Amon had just left so I didn't think much of it when I asked Aiden to meet me at the park across the street to talk. Oh yeah, and I needed him to bring me some grub from the all night club that served chicken wings twenty-four hours a damn day. Those motherfuckers were always fresh.

"Why can't I just come over your mom's? You're asking me to drive all the way over to the Southside to talk?" Aiden asked sounding as if he was suspicious about why I chose the meeting spot that I did.

"Are you gonna meet me there or not?"

"I'll be there in thirty minutes," he replied hastily.

"I'll be there waiting," I hummed as I jumped off the line and showered.

For some reason I was feeling sexy. I knew that I couldn't wear anything too revealing in the stomach area. Searching my walk-in closet from one end to the other, I came out with a flowing sleeveless blue blouse and a pair of Capri leggings.

I snapped on my earrings and sprayed some smell good. I called him to see where he was. As usual, he was right on time….

"Hello?"

"Where are you?" Aiden laughed.

"No, where are you?" I giggled as I stepped out into the crisp night air. Froze my chi-chi's right away and had my nipples sticking up at attention.

"I'm coming down the block," he revealed. "I'll be there in three minutes.

I hurried to get over there before he could see which house I was coming out of. Those days a bitch couldn't get away with nothing.

"Ooooo Weeee," Aiden exclaimed with his hand over his mouth as he approached me. "You are looking hella fine tonight ma."

That shit turned my face red and I couldn't help but blush. "Thanks Aiden."

"No, shit, I'm ready to thank your mama," he teased as he came to kiss my cheek. "You look like you gettin' a little thick there baby."

"You calling me fat?" I snapped trying to pull from his hold when I saw the set of headlights approaching.

Slowly sliding out of the bright beams shining from the park lights, I hid behind the awning a bit.

"Are you hiding from someone?" Aiden asked as he followed my line of sight.

I was so busy watching Amon's car drive by a few times, that I couldn't concentrate on shit Aiden was saying. It was all a big blur...

"Can I call you later Aiden?" I requested as I waited for Amon's car to turn the corner yet another time. "That's my mother and I don't want her to create a scene."

"Aint you grown?" Aiden teased as I walked him to his car. "I don't know what ya sneaky ass is up to Ty'Keisha, but I'm gonna find out! Just watch and see."

Soon as I got Aiden to pull off, I rushed across the street to the house I shared with Amon. The second I slid the key in the lock, that nigga was pulling up in the driveway.

I stood there frozen until he got out of the car and came close to me.

"What the fuck you got on and who the fuck was that you were talking to across the street Ty?" Amon questioned through clinched teeth, but I could still smell the scent of Jack Daniels Honey.

That time I didn't have an answer for him. I was tired of coming up with a damn lie...

Amon Rivers

Ty thought her little ass was slick. Now I didn't see who she was talking to in the car across the street but I could tell it was a nigga. "If this bitch is playing games with me I swear on my mama it's gonna be some shit!"

I already had people talking shit saying that if Ty was pregnant that she wasn't as far along as she said she was. I had yet to go to a doctor's appointment, see an ultrasound picture or anything. It was frustrating as hell.

At first the idea of being someone's father scared the shit out of me. I was only a young teenager when Ty told me about the baby. Then all the shit happened with Twan and next thing I knew, three and a half months had flown by.

Now according to my calculations and what Ty told me, she had to be around six months pregnant. When I asked her about why she didn't make an ultrasound appointment, she gave me some shit about not wanting to know the sex of the baby until it was born. To say that I was mad was an understatement. That's just why I bounced on her ass.

I wasn't even gone for too long before I decided to go back home. I caught her ass the first time I rolled down the block but I didn't say shit until we were in the house. She had some explaining to do.

"So you ain't got shit to say Ty?"

"What you want me to say Amon? Someone spoke so I spoke back. I'm not a rude ass like you."

"Rude huh? The fuck was you doing outside any damn way?"

"I needed some fucking air. Is that ok with you Dad?"

"Shorty you got some shit with you and you really testing a nigga right now, I swear. Who the fuck was in that car?"

"I already told you Amon. Someone spoke so I spoke back. Can't you hear?"

I didn't even bother to say shit else to Ty. I just turned around and went into the other bedroom. I wasn't gonna spend all night arguing with her ass. It seemed like that's all we did since she found out she was pregnant. My patience was running thin with her overly emotional ass.

While I was laying there listening to her crying in the other room I got more pissed off. Some shit still wasn't right and I knew the one person who could fix it. I slid my phone out my pocket and called the one woman I could always depend on. My mama.

"Hey Ma," I greeted when she finally answered the phone.

"Hey son what's cracking?"

"Ma you can't be answering the phone like that. You ain't cool like that," I clowned laughing at her attempt.

"Boy bye! I was cool before you even knew what being cool was. Now what do you want? You only call when something is wrong."

"You're right. It's about Ty. I think she lying to me."

"About her being pregnant? Well you know, I was at the store the other day and ran into that lil friend of hers, La Cucaracha or whatever her name is. That chick got that ratchet ass name, but it fits her perfectly. Anyway, she told me that she saw Ty at a clinic and overheard her telling another girl that she wasn't but about four or five months pregnant or something like that. Ain't she 'posed to be further than that?"

"What?" I snapped.

"Same shit I said. Now what you need to do is bring her to mama and lemme see if I can get it out of her. You know I can smell bullshit from a mile away boy. Bring her around here tomorrow."

"Aight Ma."

"And son?"

"Yeah Ma?"

"Don't do shit to that girl tonight cuz I know your temper. Just let me handle her. Promise me that."

"Aight Ma, I promise. I love you."

"Love you too."

After hanging up with my mom I was pissed. I knew it! I really wanted to storm into that room and throw her ass down the stairs. If what my mama said was true then it was gonna be a problem. I tried to go to sleep but I couldn't.

I threw my stuff back on, snatched up my keys and left. I couldn't stay in that house with Ty that night because if I did, I was going hurt her. I hopped in my whip and peeled out of there so fast it wasn't even funny.

I hit the block and who was the first person I saw? La'Karata with her ratchet ass. I wanted to avoid her but at the same time I wanted to know if what she told my mama was true. I parked and hopped out.

"Yo La'Karata!" I yelled in her direction. She looked up when she heard me yell her name and walked towards me with a goofy ass smile on her face. She put an extra switch in her hips and sashayed her ass right up to me.

"Hey Amon boo. How you been?"

"Fuck all that shit. I heard you told my moms' some bullshit. Why you running your mouth?"

"About Ty? Nigga please! You just mad because you don't wanna believe that ya girl is a bust down. Just admit the shit and move on my nigga."

"You know what? You got a lot of mouth on you for a female. I swear you don't know when to shut the fuck up."

"Yeah I got a whole lot of mouth but I know how to do something with it too. You should let me show you some time."

I can't even lie. When she said that shit my dick immediately stood up. I hadn't had any sex in a minute either. My man was begging to be freed from behind my zipper but I tried to hide that shit. She saw it before I could. It was too late.

"Looks like ya man wanna see what my mouth do. What's up?"

"Naw shorty it ain't even like---,"

Before I could even finish my sentence she shoved me into the darkened alley near where we were standing. In less than a minute she was down on her knees with my dick in her mouth. *I couldn't even front, that shit was 'good than a muthafucka'.* I let her keep going until I busted a fat ass nut down her throat. She savored every single drop and licked me clean.

"Damn La, I ain't know you was putting it down like that. Ima have to come back and check you out."

"Yeah you say that shit now Amon, but we'll see. You know where I'm at."

I didn't say shit as she reapplied her lip gloss like nothing happened. Damn lil mama had that Karrine Steffans super head. I needed more of that. Against my better judgment, I decided that I'd be getting up with her again.

I hopped back in my whip feeling a little off, but I shook it. Shit, I saw no reason for me to feel guilty about it. I needed to bust that nut. It was the perfect thing to help me go to sleep.

I drove back home feeling tired and full of yawns. I would definitely be going to sleep when I got in. It only took about thirty minutes. I went right in the guest bedroom and headed straight to bed.

****

I woke up the next morning feeling like a million bucks. I jumped in the shower and washed up. Ty didn't know it yet, but after today her ass was going back to live with her mama. I couldn't deal with a trifling broad. I had too much at stake.

Once I was fresh and dressed, I went to find Ty. I found her in the kitchen cooking breakfast. She barely acknowledged my presence. I was cool with that though. I was feeling great.

"Yo lil mama I need you to get dressed."

"For?"

"I'm taking you to meet my mama. Since we having a baby and shit, I figured she would need to know who you were."

"What I need to meet yo mama for? I ain't having a baby with her."

Before I could even think about what I was doing I had Ty's lil ass hemmed up against the wall. I was so fucking pissed at her lack of respect for my mother.

Her dangling feet were kicking at my shin and that's when I noticed she was turning blue in the face. I dropped her ass to the floor.

"Man Ty, yo old disrespectful ass. Just get the fuck up and do what I say. All that smart mouth shit is gonna get you fucked up. I ain't never put my hands on a female before, but you pushing it!"

"Fuck you Amon! I ain't going nowhere with ya ass."

"Either you get up and do what I said or get the fuck out my house. Your choice but you got 30 minutes to make it."

I left Ty gasping for air on the kitchen floor as I walked off. I took a seat in the living room and waited the half hour I had given her. Promptly twenty-five minutes later Ty was standing at the entrance to the living room leering at me.

I paid her ass no mind as I got up and walked towards the door. She followed behind just like I knew she would and walked over to the car as I locked the house up. I hit the alarm and she pulled her door open, got in the car and slammed it with way too much attitude for me. I didn't give a shit though. Today was judgment day for her ass anyway.

We rode silently to my mama's house and pulled up shortly after leaving our own spot. I got out and gave her ass a look that told her to try me if she wanted to. She got in gear and got her ass out the car.

Once again she followed behind me as we made it to the door. I rang the bell and waited for my mother to answer.

"Why hello son, Ty'Keisha. Come in."

My mama stepped back and allowed us to enter. From the smell of things she had cooked and I was hungry as hell. *I know you're probably thinking, why I didn't eat the breakfast Ty cooked but like I said, I didn't trust her. That included her cooking.*

I let my nose lead me to the kitchen and was helping myself to a plate when the ladies walked in. I didn't say a thing. I just watched how they interacted with each other. They sat at the kitchen table and began to converse.

"So Ty'Keisha, Amon told me that y'all are having a baby. How far along are you?"

"I just made six months yesterday."

"When are you due?"

"March 13th ma'am."

"Don't ma'am me honey. Call me Ma because you are having my grandbaby. Lemme ask you something though."

"Yeah, sure. You can ask me anything."

"If you're so far along then why are you so small? What did the doctors have to say about that? From the looks of it I'd say you're no more than about three months."

I saw her flinch at my mother's question and that was what I was waiting for. She started shifting nervously in her chair and avoided looking at me. She did however, answer my mother.

"The doctor said she wasn't too concerned because not everyone gains weight the same way. I'll probably just pick it up in the next couple of weeks or so. I'm really not worried."

"I think you need one of them ultrasound thingy's."

"Naw, I'll wait."

"Ok honey. Well if there's anything you need then feel free to call me."

"Will do Ms. Riv- I mean Ma."

I didn't say anything and neither did my mama. She just gave me a look. It was an expression that made me know that she would be calling me later. I trusted my mama so whatever she was going to tell me was law.

Ty'Keisha

It was one fucking thing after another. My shit was falling apart and a bitch had some serious gluing to do. First, the shit with Amon catching me outside talking to Aiden had me busted. Then, the little trip to his mother's for an interrogation topped shit off. That was it.

"Why are you doing all this Amon?" I questioned the moment we made it back home. "I feel like you don't believe me."

"Oh, I believe you baby," he smirked as he took his ass back in the extra bedroom dialing someone on his cell. He closed the door behind him and began to have a conversation.

I didn't chase behind him. I needed time to think.

I knew my ass was on the verge of desperation so I began to plot to keep my man. I had to think of something.

"Yeah man, I'm on my way." I could hear Amon say as he walked by the bedroom. "Let me see if Ty wants to go."

My heart began beating fast in anticipation, especially when I saw that big grin on my man's face. "What's up?"

"It's this little get together tonight," he began while pulling out a wad of money. "Take this and go get your hair and nails done. Get you a new fit too baby."

"For real?" I shouted excitely.

"Yeah, now I gotta make a few runs. Meet me back here no later than 9 tonight."

"I'll be here. Thanks baby."

Before I could hug and kiss all over Amon, that nigga was out the door. "Shit"

Focusing in on the bankroll he had just handed me, I began to count the bills. When I finished, the total was five thousand dollars.

Traveling to the garage, I went to add it to my stash. Ever since Amon and I had moved in together, I had been saving my money. Knowing that I was on shaky ground, I had to have a cushion to fall back on.

Hurrying back inside, I went to my room. I went directly to the oversized walk-in closet. I went to my side and pulled out something comfortable to wear. Within the next twenty minutes I was in the wind...

First stop was the hair shop on Roosevelt Avenue. They knew how to hook a mean weave up. When I came out of there my shit was down to the middle of my back and flowing with curls. "Flyy"

Next I had to visit the Korean's down on 1st Ave. I hated to fuck with them because they always started speaking in their language then look at you and laugh. I knew those sneaky motherfuckers where cracking on my feet, but I didn't give a damn. "Just hook my shit up and shut the hell up with all that jibber-jabber shit!"

"Flower for you?"

"Hell naw! Did I ask for a flower?"

I swear those fools ask the same shit every time and get the same answer. "I'm gonna learn how to say 'no and don't ask me again' in Korean the first chance I get!"

"You want your eyebrows done?"

"For real?"

"Yes, I make pretty for you," she smiled.

"No," I snapped. "You understand that shit huh?"

I couldn't get out of there quick enough. I hopped in my ride and headed to the mall.

"Ring, ring"

"Hello?"

"Baby, where are you?" Amon questioned as if he was up to something. "It's almost seven."

"I'll be there within the hour," I answered.

I only needed a pair of black wedges to go with this new fit I had picked up the week before. I had to hide all that shit in the spare bedroom in the back of the small closet.

In and out of the mall within thirty minutes was a record for me. I was anxious to get home to get ready to enjoy an evening with my man. That was my chance to set things right and get my relationship back on the proper track.

When I got to the house I found the alarm off. That was real unusual for Amon not to have that shit set. He kept that shit on twenty-four-seven.

Creeping inside, I slid my keys in my purse and set it down on the table in the foyer.

"There's a meeting in my bedroom...," sang out from the speakers.

That shit was louder than normal and caught my attention right away. My senses had been on high alert ever since I actually got pregnant.

As I continued down the hallway, I caught the scent of strawberries. The closer I got, the stronger the smell was.

"Oh, my baby getting ready for me!" I whispered excitedly as I stripped out of all of my clothes.

After setting them on the floor outside the bedroom, I eased the door open and entered the dimly lit room. As I crept nearer to the bed that was positioned on the far wall, I could see two bodies intertwined.

"What the hell?" I yelled out and flicked on the light forgetting all about that I was without clothes. "For real Amon?"

"Who's she?" The ghetto bitch with the big tits and fake ass. "Is she coming to join us? She's pregnant!"

"Where the fuck are your clothes?" Amon laughed.

"You got me fucked up! I'm taking my shit and leaving!"

"Bye," Amon clowned as he continued spooning with the bitch in our bed.

I rushed to the closet to get my shit and found my side of the closet empty.

"Where's my shit?"

"In the garage all packed the fuck up!" he continued to show out. "You and that niggas baby can get to steppin'. You thought you was playin' me? Nah shorty, you was playin' yourself. No hard feelings though. I even let you keep your little stash you had out there."

I couldn't even answer that sneaky motherfucker. He was two steps ahead of the game and I could only be mad at myself for getting caught slipping, but now my feelings were involved. I wasn't about to go out like that. He wasn't about to just quit me.

"This is your fucking baby Amon but if this is what you want, I'm gone."

I got dressed and stomped to the garage in tears. The vision of him and that bitch in our bed wouldn't leave my mind. The more I thought about it, the more I wanted revenge.

"Let me get my shit before I beat that bitch's ass and get locked the hell up!" I huffed as I loaded my car little by little.

When I finished, I snuck back in the house and got the nine Amon had hidden in the kitchen. I removed the safety and went to the room where I caught them fucking.

"Pop, Pop"

I put one bullet in the wall and the next one in the headboard.

The bitch jumped up out of the bed as if she was on steroids. She came straight for me and knocked me onto the floor. She jumped on top of my pregnant belly and we began fighting.

"Bitch you got me fucked up!" I yelled out as I rolled her up off of me and began to beat her ass.

Amon stood there butt naked laughing. He was even cheering the bitch on. That did nothing but make me go harder, pregnant and all...

"Pop"

"Get the fuck off of her and get out!" Amon yelled out after releasing a round in the air. "This is your last warning!"

When I didn't budge, he picked me up off of my feet and carried me out kicking and screaming. He didn't put me down until we got outside.

"Fuck you!"

"No fuck you!"

Amon laughed as he rushed inside and set the alarm. I rushed to disarm it, only to find out that he changed the code.

"Little bitch!"

I picked up the biggest rock I could hold and heaved it through the front bay window. The crash sent the alarm wild.

"Take that!"

I hopped in my car and peeled out feeling justified. I had my money, my car and my shit.

"I'll just get a weekly on the south side," I decided as I directed my ride onto the highway.

When I got there I was too tired to carry shit, so I grabbed a few things along with my cash box and went inside to check in.

"How much for the week?"

"$1,200"

Digging into my box, I found one stack of bills with a note.

"Did you think you were really going to step up out of here with fifteen G's? The only reason I'm leaving you this little 5K is on GP. I feel sorry for the kid and your dumb ass. Have a good life and stay the fuck away from me."

I shook my head as I paid for fourteen days. My money was limited and now I had to come up with yet another plan. Amon was not getting off that damn easy. I knew way too much about his illegal dealings. If I had to get dirty, I wasn't about to hesitate...

Amon Rivers

Ty's ass thought she was slick but I knew how to play her little game. After moms' hollered at me and told me that she did not think Ty was pregnant by me that was it. I was not going to get stuck taking care of no other dude's baby. That was for damn sure.

The chick who was in the crib with me when Ty got there was a bitch I used to fuck. When I came at her she jumped at the chance to get with me again. She didn't need to know that I was using her ass. Then again, I didn't even think she cared. Little did she know, what we just finished doing wasn't going past that night.

After sexing ol' girl crazy again, I told her to bounce. Yeah she had a little attitude or whatever but I didn't even care. Her job was done...

Weeks passed and I stayed grinding. I avoided women all together. That lasted all of a month. By then I was restless and had to get some pussy.

"I'm gonna hit up the party," I thought aloud as I hopped in the shower and got myself dressed.

By ten o'clock, I was pulling up at my homeboy's house. It was a pretty decent gathering. The drinks were on hit and there were plenty of women to go around. I dapped up a few people before going to make a cocktail.

As I was pouring myself a cup of Grey Goose I felt a pair of hands slip around my waist and down the front of my jeans. I quickly pulled the unknown hands away from me and turned around. That was when I saw La'Karata standing there.

I had to admit she was looking damn good. The fitted maxi dress she had on was hugging her curves as if it was painted on. I wondered if I could get some more of her bomb ass head again.

"Yo La, what's going on?"

"You."

"Oh me huh? What you getting at?"

"How bout you let me holla at you bout that upstairs?"

"Ok bet."

I grabbed my drink and followed behind her as I watched her big butt bounce up and down. We found a vacant bedroom as soon as we reached the top of the stairs.

It was like as soon as the door was closed she was all over me. I could barely say or do anything because she was on it. Before she could get a word in I had my dick in her mouth.

Shit, I barely could speak a word my damn self. I could only utter sounds due to the broad sucking my dick like her life depended on it. I thought the shit was good the first time but this time it was even better. I gripped the back of La'Karata's head and started pumping faster and faster.

It didn't matter what I did, she just kept on taking it. Before I knew it, I was busting a big ass nut down her throat. She swallowed it all just like before. It was over just as quick as it started and I went right back to doing me as if I didn't even know the chick.

I had gotten so smashed at the party that I didn't even know how I got home. All I knew was that I rolled over and saw that it was almost one in the afternoon, by what the digital clock said on the cable box. I sat up slowly in bed because I had a banging headache. That's when I noticed that I wasn't in bed alone.

A snoring La'Karata lay next to me sleeping peacefully. I didn't wanna wake her up but she had no choice; she had to go. I shook her awake and told her that I had some shit to handle. She didn't fuss or argue with me. She got up, put her stuff on and stood by the front door waiting patiently for me.

I got myself together in less than fifteen minutes and was ready to go. I quickly dropped her off at her spot but not before she told me some important information. I knew then that I had made the right decision to fuck with her one last time.

Just when I started feeling bad for fucking with her or doing what I did to Ty, I got hit with that reality check. She wasn't a clingy chick and she proved that shit.

When we pulled up in front of her spot, she just jumped out without so much as a fight. If she kept this shit up, then I might just stay fucking with her. I didn't know though. I knew how her ass could get. Right then I could not deal with it. I had business that was more pressing.

I hit the block and checked on a few spots before I decided to drive down Division to go to DJ's. To me it was the best place in town to get a pizza puff with fries and mild sauce. I parked and went inside. Lo and behold, I ran smack into Ty. I was gonna turn around and leave but I said fuck it.

"Damn nigga I know you can see my big, pregnant ass? You don't know how to speak to yo baby mama?"

"Yeah I would, if I had one."

I had to admit, her stomach was getting big and she looked every bit of seven months, maybe even further.

"Fuck you mean Amon? You know good and damn well this is your baby."

"Oh word? I do? Then who the fuck is Aiden?"

The look on her face told me all I needed to know. She started stuttering and trying to talk but I didn't even care. What she was trying to say was irrelevant anyway. I ordered, got my food and as I was walking out Ty ran over and grabbed my arm.

"Shorty if you know what's good for you then you'll take your hands off me."

"Amon please, let me explain. It's not what you think it is."

"Not what I think huh? Then why when I mentioned this Aiden cat you shut up? Nothing to say now huh? Man Ty carry yo ass on!"

I roughly pulled my arm out her grasp and walked towards my car. I took one last look at who I thought was my ride or die before getting in my car and pulling away. I was glad I found out the truth before the baby got here because had I found out afterwards, that baby woulda been without a mother.

Ty'Keisha

My ass was fucking speechless when Amon busted me up about Aiden. I couldn't believe he knew.

"How did he find out?" I wondered as I tried to save face and rush out to my car in tears.

Everything that I had planned had gone to shit. Yeah, I could have called Aiden and had him take care of me, but hell, as far as I knew he was still living with his parents his damn self. I wanted Amon…

As I sat in my ride, I drew out my cell and began dialing his phone. He sent my call straight to his voicemail, which was full as usual. I had no choice but to text him.

Just as I was about to send my message, I noticed that I was parked directly across from Amon's car. My sneaky ass began to plot right away.

Taking the water bottle that sat beside me, I doused some drops on my head, face and down between my legs. I messed my hair up and ripped my clothes a bit.

I knew that what I was about to do was a desperate move, but I was fresh out of ideas. I needed to get Amon to feel sorry for me so I could get close to him again. I knew that he still had to have some type of love for me. He had too…

Waiting patiently for the next ten minutes, I finally spotted Amon coming out of the side door. I eased out my car and began moaning loudly.

"Someone help me!"

"What the fuck?" Amon gasped as he ran up to me.

"Someone just tried to rob me and I think my water broke!" I lied pointing to the north side of the parking lot. "I think I need to go to the hospital."

Man, I was laying it on thick. Shit, I was impressing myself!

"Let me call you an ambulance Ty," Amon suggested as he held my body up.

"No, I don't want to wait."

When I saw that he wasn't quite buying it, I began crying and getting angry.

"That's okay! I can drive myself!"

Right when I turned around, I began to fake a labor pain. I knew it was too early, but that was the only card I had left to play.

"Ugh," I shouted as I allowed my body to hit the ground. I made sure to protect my stomach on the way down.

"Ty!"

I heard him, but I faked like I blacked out. I had his ass panicking like a motherfucker. The shit was so damn funny that I almost burst out in laughter.

After struggling to get me back on my feet, Amon began to shake me. I open my eyes just a bit then squinted.

"What happened?"

"Ya ass needs to go to the hospital," Amon spat as he started walking me to his car. "I have some questions for the doctor myself, since you don't wanna tell a nigga shit."

My blood pressure shot upward as my body trembled. My plan was not only falling apart in my face, the motherfucker was backfiring. I had to think quickly.

"Let's go to the urgent care clinic down the street. It's closer," I suggested as Amon helped me in his ride.

My homegirl Tammy worked in that one and I knew I could pay her to come in the room and maybe throw some false information in the air. I sent her a text to make sure she was there.

"Yes," I thought as she hit me back telling me that she was there for another two hours.

"What's up Ty?" Amon inquired with a suspicious expression. "You texting folks and shit, you must be alright!"

"No, I'm not okay, but sitting here crying about it aint gonna make it no better. I aint no punk."

"Yeah, I aint either!" Amon muffled under his breath as we arrived at the clinic.

When we entered, I bent over a bit and held onto my stomach. When the nurse saw me, she rushed and asked did I need a transport to the hospital.

"I don' fucked up now!" I thought trying to play it off.

"Maybe she does," Amon smirked.

"Can you just check me and then if I need to go I will." I snapped.

I was beginning to get irritated. I wanted to know where the hell Tammy was. I could not text her again because Amon was all up in my grill watching my every fucking move.

"Ma'am, we can take you back right now," the nurse shouted through the glass window. "He can go back with you if he wants."

"Bitch, did I ask you that shit?" I screamed in my mind. I really wanted to stick my hand in that little hole and snatch her ass up.

"Oh, I can?" Amon perked up. "Cool, yeah, I wanna go back."

I forced a smile and prayed that I saw a familiar face at any moment.

"We need to get you straight to the ultrasound room to see what's going on with the baby," the assistant informed me as she took my vitals. "Everything is good on this end."

"Thank you," I sighed as I rubbed my tummy.

Soon as we got to the end of the hallway and passed the nurses desk, I spotted my friend. Thing was, so did Amon.

"Aye, what's good wit ya Tammy?" he greeted with a hug. "Ty, you know my cousin DJ's girl Tammy?"

"Huh?"

That was it. I was all out of ammo...

Amon Rivers

I didn't know what the connection was between Ty and Tammy but I caught the shocked expression on Ty's face when I said that Tammy was DJ's girl. If she thought she was about to be on bullshit then she had me fucked up.

Tammy was like family because she had been with DJ since as long as I could remember. I made a mental note to hit her up later and have a talk with her. I asked Tammy what room we were going to and she told us to follow her.

Ty followed closely behind Tammy and I brought up the rear. I wanted nothing more than to knock the shit out of her but I still had a little bit of feelings for her. Call me crazy, but I was starting to love little mama until she pulled the bullshit with the baby. I really wanted to believe it was mine but she fucked up.

Tammy showed us into the examination room and told Ty to undress from the waist down. She handed her a gown and told us that someone would be in shortly. I turned my back to Ty as she undressed. I didn't want her ass to get the wrong impression for nothing. I was only there because even though I had all the signs, including what my mom said, I still needed confirmation.

"I don't know why you have your back turned Amon. It ain't like you never saw me naked before."

"Yeah but before you was my shorty, now you just somebody that I used to give a fuck about."

"Damn Amon, that's cold."

"Naw, that's real lil mama."

Just as she was about to answer me there was a knock on the door and the doctor came in. I had a ton of questions but I thought it would be best if I just sat there quietly. I knew there was no way that Ty could lie to a medical professional about her pregnancy. There were just too many ways that he could figure shit out. I waited for either one of them to speak.

"Hello folks. My name is Dr. Perla and I'll be attending to you this evening. What brought you in today young lady?"

"Well doc I was getting into my car when somebody tried to rob me. There was a struggle. I was knocked down and hit in the stomach. I think my water broke and I'm worried about my baby. My boyfriend happened to see me and brought me in."

"Well ok let's get you checked out and make sure you're both alright. I'll call for an ultrasound technician as soon as I check your cervix."

Ty thought she was slick with that boyfriend comment but I let it go for the time being. I watched as the doctor washed her hands before putting on a pair of latex gloves. She tore open a package of lubricant and spread it on her fingers before checking Ty's cervix. I watched and waited to see what the doctor had to say.

"Hmmm well it feels a little like your cervix is softening, so let me make that call."

She threw her gloves away and washed her hands before leaving out the room.

"If yo slick ass calls me ya boyfriend one more time I can guarantee yo ass will go into labor right the fuck now."

"It ain't like I was lying. You used to be mine."

"Yeah used to be; as in not anymore! Don't fuck with me Ty."

Again just as she was about to say something there was a knock at the door. In walked an extremely happy, mousy type of chick. She came to wheel Ty into the ultrasound room. Shit, I was right along with them.

"Hi I'm Sarah and I'll be the technician that will be checking on mom and baby today. If you'll please just lay back and pull your gown up over your belly we can get started."

Ty did as she was told and the tech started her exam. She spread some type of gel on her stomach and used what looked like a small microphone to roll over Ty's belly. I watched her hit button after button and take measurements of the baby without saying a word. I figured now was as good a time as any to start asking questions.

"Sarah, can you tell me what the sex of the baby is?"

"Sure can! Mom is that ok with you?"

Ty just shook her head and didn't say shit. I think she got the point now after our little talk.

"Ok it looks like you're having a.....whoa!"

"Whoa what? Is something wrong?"

"No nothing is wrong so sorry if I scared you guys there but it looks like there are two babies here."

My eyes damn near bulged out my head and Ty was looking like she was near tears.

"Baby A looks like it's a girl and baby B is a...it's a girl as well. Congratulations!"

I watched her wipe her instrument off, along with the gel off Ty's belly before asking my last question.

"Sarah I have one last question."

"Ok shoot."

"Can you tell me how far along Ty is? Her OB gave us conflicting dates as to when she was due and I just want us to be prepared."

"No problem Dad. It looks like Mom is measuring right around 26 weeks. The babies are healthy and weighing just what they should be weighing. I could be off a little. With twins it can be a bit complicated?"

That was enough information for me to think Ty was lying. She should have been at least a little over seven months because that last time I knew I pulled out! I didn't give a damn about the complicated shit that Sarah was talking about.

"Is there anything else?"

"No ma'am that will be all. You've been a great help, thank you."

"No problem. I'll let the doctor know my results and she'll be back in with you shortly. Have a goodnight y'all."

I waited until Sarah the Tech was gone before I turned to Ty. She really was trying to trap me with another nigga's kids. She wasn't just having one baby but two and had tried to pass them off on me. She must've thought I was some lame ass nigga who would just believe her. One thing my mama didn't raise was a fool.

"So you really ain't having my baby and was gonna lie to me Ty? That's some foul ass shit lil mama. You have a nice life and call ya real baby daddy for a ride home. I'm out."

"For real?" Ty asked sounding dumbfounded. "You heard what she said! Her calculations may be off!"

"For real!"

I chucked the deuces at lil mama and left. I saw Tammy on the way out and told her to let me know anything else she might find out about Ty. She assured me that she would and I left. I strolled to my car happy as hell that I dodged that bullet. After all the conniving ass shit Ty did, I didn't want to ever be tied to that bitch for life.

Ty'Keisha

My whole plan went to shit and I couldn't blame anyone but myself. I had backed myself so far in a corner that I had no choice but to call up Aiden, but I needed to talk to Tammy first.

"Damn bitch! I thought you had my back?"

"Bitch you didn't say yo ass was playing the game with Amon! That's DJ's cousin!"

"So?"

"So, that's my man and I'm not jeopardizing my relationship so you can have one!"

"Bitch, you should have made a better decision!"

"Say what?" Tammy huffed stepping out of her comfort zone just like I wanted her too.

"You heard me bitch!" I spat daring her to do something.

"Pop"

The bitch hit me with a right hook in the jaw. I took that shit like a champ and fell out on the floor acting a damn fool.

"Oh my God!" I screamed and started with the dramatics. "This nurse hit me!"

"What?" Tammy shouted looking confused as the security guards rushed her.

"What type of clinic are you running up in here?" I continued with the charade. "I'm gonna sue you up the ass!"

Some older looking white woman rushed the situation. "Are you okay Ma'am?"

"No," I grunted as I held on to my stomach and moaned. "I'm cramping, but I don't want to be seen here! I don't feel safe!"

"Don't worry Ma'am. Security is going to escort Ms. Thomas out of the building and trespass her off of the property. I promise you, you'll be safe. If I have to see to it myself!"

"Bitch it's not over!" Tammy shouted out as she was lifted off of her feet and taken towards the nearest exit.

"Oh yeah bitch, it's over!" I mouthed towards Tammy with a sneaky grin.

After she was gone, I straightened my clothes out and grabbed my handbag.

"I wouldn't be seen again in this place if my life depended it on it!" I shouted at the top of my lungs. "You'll be hearing from my lawyer!"

I left the clinic and headed directly to the nearest hospital to get checked out. I told them what had happened and they sent an officer to me to give a statement. I made sure to name Tammy as the assailant.

Once I was finished and waiting to be released, I dialed the only person that I knew would have my back after I did some dumb shit. Aiden...

"Hey, I know I've been avoiding you, but there's a reason," I began.

"It's okay Ty'Keisha, just let me know where you are." Aiden fussed sounding concerned.

When I told him that I was at the hospital, he began to flip out. He wanted to know why I was just now calling him.

"Are you gonna come?" I whined laying it on thick.

"Yeah, I'll be there in twenty."

I hung up feeling a little better, but I still wasn't ready to give up on Amon. I knew there just had to be enough love left to give me another chance. If not, there was always plan B. That was to fuck up his whole world, beginning with his business...

****

Aiden showed up right on time. Right as they were handing me my discharge papers he rushed me. His eyes traveled directly down to my stomach.

"What's going on?" he asked in a panicked tone still staring downward. "Are you alright?"

"Yes," I smirked as I handed him the proof of pregnancy. He skimmed over the paperwork then looked up at me.

"What, pregnant with twins?" Aiden shouted as he read the documents over twice. "How long have you known?"

There was a pause in the conversation and I had to gather my thoughts before answering him.

"I had a feeling that I was, but I wasn't sure until my stomach started cramping earlier." I lied. "I was scared to tell you because I didn't know how you were gonna react."

"I don't know why baby," he smiled and gently rubbed my tummy. "You know I love you and I'm here for you."

"But I don't have anywhere to go Aiden!"

"You can come home with me," he suggested.

"I can't live with you and your parent's baby," I smirked knowing good and well that I wasn't going for that shit.

"If you called a nigga you would know I had my own spot," he smiled sounding a little gangster. That shit was turning me on.

"So, you have enough room for us?"

"Girl, if you don't bring yo ass on."

My mind was so confused. The Aiden I thought I knew wasn't the one that showed up at the hospital to pick me up. He was on some other shit and I liked it.

"Ty'Keisha, let me be up front and tell you that I know about you fucking with Amon. Your homegirl that lived upstairs from you made sure she told me that. Hell, it only took a hundred dollars to make her ass talk." Aiden blurted out with no shame. "The only thing I want to know is, are you sure these babies are mine?"

"Yes, one hundred percent sure," I answered unknowingly without entertaining his comments pertaining to Amon. "Are you in or naw?"

"Am I in what?"

"Are you in this shit for the long haul or do you just wanna be here for the babies? Honest answer please..."

"Like I said, I love you baby. You just have to start being honest with me. Like this shit with Amon. I need to know what's up with that situation before we can establish anything stable between us, cool?"

"Cool"

Aiden clinched my hand as we left the hospital. We chopped it up as we headed to his three bedroom home in an upscale neighborhood on the east side. I can't lie. I was in total shock when we pulled up to his estate. That shit put Amon's place to shame...

I entered and made myself right at home. Aiden began waiting on me hand and foot. As nice as it was, I still couldn't get revenge off my mind. I just had to get back at Amon. Even if it was the last thing I did.

If I couldn't have him, no one could...

Amon Rivers

I left the hospital and Ty's ass in an upbeat mood. I was happy as hell that I wasn't the father of her kids. Kids, can you believe that shit? The bitch was having twins but they weren't mine. I was in such a good mood that I decided to hit up La'Karata and see if she wanted to chill with me that night.

I was starting to grow fond of lil mama because she wasn't like Ty. She didn't nag or complain about anything. When I told her ass to do something, she did it with no problems. Make no mistakes about it though. I wasn't trying to go down that road again with anyone.

I shot her a quick text and she responded back a few minutes later asking me what time to be ready. I hit her back and told her I'd pick her up at eight and she said ok. Now that I had my night settled it was time for me to hit my sheets.

Fucking with Ty I didn't get home till almost six in the morning so I needed a few hours of sleep before I could function. I wasn't even all the way in the bed good enough before DJ hit my line. I started not to pick up but then I thought about it.

"It could be something about business." I went ahead and answered.

"Yo Cuz everything straight?"

"Naw man! Yo bitch got my bitch fired."

I made out some shuffling in the background. I could hear Tammy's voice. She was going off on DJ about calling her a bitch.

"I ain't gon' be too many bitches right now DJ. I'm not in the mood for this shit."

I laughed about that shit until I heard DJ get back on the line.

"Man that bitch Ty provoked Tammy at her job. She was talking shit about how Tammy didn't have her back and whatnot. You know how Tammy got a temper and shit so I guess Ty took shit too far. Anyway Tammy fucked around and punched the bitch in her jaw so they fired her. I don't know about you Cuz but ima hurt that ho' when I catch her, pregnant or not."

"Ha damn Tammy's still the same I see. Check it out though; I don't give two fucks about that lying ass bitch or what y'all do to her. As far as I'm concerned she's dead to me. My nigga, the bitch wasn't even pregnant by me. The doctor confirmed that shit." I stretched the truth hoping I was right.

"Word? Well ok then. I wanted to give you a heads-up because I knew you used to fuck with her little ass but now it's all good. Appreciate that Cuz."

"Already."

After I hung up with DJ I just laughed. I couldn't believe that Tammy popped Ty's ass. I was just mad that I wasn't there to see that shit. Oh well, that was her own fault.

I settled into my bed and dozed off almost instantly.

****

Hours later, I jumped up with a hard dick and sweating like a slave. I went to relieve myself and decided to hop in the shower. While I was in there, I thought about what I had dreamt before I woke up.

I was in bed, but it wasn't in my house. I had this bad bitch riding me reverse cowgirl and she was going to work. It wasn't until she looked back at me that I realized it was Milagros. I don't know why I was dreaming about her all of a sudden but her offer never stayed gone from my mind too long.

I wanted to be a king but I didn't think I had quite made it there yet. Besides, Milagros wasn't one to play games with who she was fucking. I knew she'd be playing for keeps so I decided not to get with her until I was ready for it.

I stroked my dick while I was in the shower thinking about Milagros' sexy ass. That was the best nut I had busted in a while too.

I finished washing up so I could hit the streets before getting up with La'Karata later. I needed to check on my money because as the saying went, 'business is always first'.

I got dressed in some black Nike sweats, a plain black tee and some all black Air Force Ones. I threw my Nike hoodie over my head, grabbed my keys, cell and wallet before heading out the door.

Jumping in my ride, I was feeling and looking good. I knew that I was guaranteed some ass so there wasn't one reason for me to try and go all out.

Next, I texted La to let her ass know I was on the way so she needed to be curbside. Not giving her a chance to reply, I headed her way.

Fifteen minutes later, I was pulling up on her block. Sure enough, she was outside waiting like a good little girl. I eased my car up beside her and she hopped in. As I veered back onto the road, I noticed she was eyeballing me from the side.

"Yo what's good ma? You cool?"

"Yeah I'm cool boo. Real cool."

"What's that supposed to mean?"

"Not right now Amon. I'm not in the mood for your shit."

"You what?" I screamed as I pulled the car over. "Man what's your malfunction La? I don't have time for bullshit tonight."

"I wanna know why you was with Ty after I told you that ho' was doing you dirty behind your back. What, her pussy that good or something?"

"Man I ain't gotta explain shit to you. Don't worry about why I was with her. As a matter of fact, how you even know about that shit?"

"Because the bitch been going around the hood since earlier telling everybody that y'all back together and shit. How you think I felt when I found out that my man was supposedly back fucking with his lying ass ex?"

"Wait a gotdamn minute! Yo who? Man? Who the fuck said we were together? You already knew what the fuck it was La so don't go getting all emotional and shit like we a couple. You gave me some head and we fucked. That's all that it is between us."

"Really Amon? So you was trying to chill tonight just so we could fuck? I haven't seen yo ass in like two weeks but I let that shit go cuz I knew you had business to handle. I was trying to show you that I wasn't like Ty's needy ass and you played me. I can't believe this shit. I got feelings too nigga!" La'Karata yelled at me.

I had to take a deep breath before I ended up with my hands around this bitch's throat. I didn't say shit while she sat there just staring at me with fire in her eyes. I didn't need that shit. All I needed was some of her fire ass head and good pussy but she was making me not even want that shit.

I busted a U-turn and rode back towards her block. When she noticed that we pulled back up in front of her spot she was pissed.

"So you don't wanna chill with me tonight now Amon?"

"Man La gone with that shit! You gotta get out."

"Fuck you Amon! I knew I should've never fucked around with yo ass!"

"Yeah but you did and now you can't take it back. Bounce shorty cuz I got shit to do."

"Now you got shit to do but you was about to chill with me. You know what? Fuck it and fuck you again Amon. Don't even bother calling me anymore."

"I sure won't. Now bounce up out my ride."

La was so mad that she hopped out my car and left the door wide open. I laughed at her childish ass as I got out to close the door while screaming at her, "Is you mad or nah?"

She replied with a middle finger as she continued to walk towards her front door. I hopped back in my ride and pulled off. After dealing with those young broads maybe it was time for me to take Milagros up on her offer.

I mean after all, if I wanted to be a king I first needed a queen right? Who better than to get with, other than thee Queen Bee herself?

I made the call as I zoomed down I-290 towards Joliet. She answered on the third ring.

"So Amon I guess you're ready now huh?"

Damn, a woman that already knew what I wanted. "That's what's up!" I thought to myself.

"Hell yeah I'm ready and I'm on the way as we speak."

"Just know that after tonight nothing will be the same. Once you're mine then you are mine. There's no going back."

"Understood my queen."

"Now hurry up and get your little sexy ass over here. I'll be waiting."

With that she hung up. Her words made my man stand at attention and he was begging to be set loose. I knew that it would be a night for me to remember forever.

"Tonight I become the king."

Ty'Keisha

Aiden and I had been kicking it for about a month or so. He was making it so hard to even think about Amon. He had been doing everything for me. He actually had me feeling loved. That was until that bitch La'Karata called me.

I started not to answer that shit, but after the fourth attempt my ass was curious. I inhaled deeply and connected the call.

"What the fuck could you possibly want you backstabbing bitch?"

"Look, I got ya bitch and I wasn't calling you for all that! You might wanna shut the fuck up and listen to what a bitch gotta say!" La'Karata spat.

"What?"

"You wanna know what Amon been up too?"

"How you gonna call me and tell me something about my man?" I huffed feeling offended.

"You know that bitch Milagros?"

"What about the bitch?"

"You know that's who that nigga is claiming now?"

"So you sayin' that Amon and that bitch are a couple?"

"That's exactly what the fuck I'm saying! Word on the street is she's daring yo ass to step to her!" La'Karata instigated. "Don't you know her family rolls deep? Don't you know that bitch aint to be played with?"

I knew exactly what La'Karata was trying to do and that shit was working. I knew how Milagros operated. I paid close attention when I was fucking with Amon. Both of those motherfuckers were in for a rude awakening.

"Well, since you wanna put yo tongue all up in the bitch's ass, ask her about me damn near running her ass over! Matter of fact, tell that bitch next time I won't miss!" I screamed before cutting her call off and dialing Amon. He answered on the first ring as if he was expecting my call.

"What the hell Ty?"

"What the hell is right! That's what I should be askin' you!"

"No, you shouldn't even be dialing my digits let alone askin' me a motherfuckin' thang bitch!"

"Bitch?"

"No, grimey ass bitch!" Amon spat and hung up on me.

I called his ass right the fuck back. He had me fucked all the way up and I was ready to tear some shit up.

"Next time you call my phone, you aint gonna like who answers the shit," Amon taunted.

"Who the Milagros bitch?"

"Bitch?"

"No, stuck up stanky ass bitch!" I replied harshly.

"I gotcha, call me back and see."

I hung up and waited a good five minutes to make sure he could round the bitch up and get her to answer his cell. I couldn't wait to verbally assassinate her ass.

"Hello?" Milagros greeted properly.

"Bitch please," I spat. "What the fuck you think answering my niggas phone is gonna do? You aint nothin' but another jump off, so join the crew."

"The crew?" she laughed. "Bitch I rides solo so don't get things misconstrued."

"Misconstrued?" I clowned. "Trick that's just what you are... Misunderstood. You's a confused bitch but I'm about to make shit very clear to you. I don't play when it comes to mine, so your best bet is to back the fuck up and know your place!"

Milagros laughed loudly and passed the phone to Amon. I could still hear her talking in the background.

"Please explain to this little girl that I will lay her body 6 feet under while she's still breathing."

"You heard that shit didn't you?" Amon clowned with a laugh. "Now that you got your warning, step the fuck off pregnant bitch! Come to think of it... You really need to watch the hell out!"

"Is this nigga threatening my seeds?" I yelled as I threw my cell into the wall.

"Who baby?" Aiden huffed as he entered the bedroom.

"Amon and his bitch," I smirked with a major attitude then lied. "He mad because I'm not having his kids and the bitch mad because the nigga won't stop calling me!"

"Don't worry Ty'Keisha. I'm about to take care of all that shit as soon as I get off my shift down at the plant." Aiden promised. "You just stay in the house and use this if you need to."

That nigga went to the closet and pulled out an oversized brief case. When he opened it up, my bottom lip dropped.

"Please don't tell me you're scared of guns baby!" Aiden questioned me with a peculiar expression.

"Naw, it's just that you seem to surprise me every damn day!" I answered in shock.

"What, you thought I was a square or some shit because I had good grades and obeyed my parents?"

"Well, uh, yeah," I admitted with a half-smile.

"Okay then, you need to come with me tonight. I'm gonna pick you up when I get off. Be ready about 2am."

"Aight, where are we going?" I asked anxiously.

"Just pick out a weapon of your choice and be ready," he smiled and kissed me on the mouth. "I have to go before my ass is late, boss or not."

"Oh shit, my baby is a Boss!"

"This aint shit baby. Wait until tonight."

When Aiden left out, I pushed the case of artillery out of the way and went in search of answers. I had to find out just how long his street ties were...

Amon Rivers

That bitch Ty was tripping for real. I knew it was a matter of time before La'Karata went and start running her mouth, which is just what I wanted her to do. She played right into my hands just like Ty's simple ass did.

I had already hipped Milagros to what was going on and she laughed at the shit. She decided to have a little fun and entertain them young broads for a second or two until Ty came at her disrespectfully. That was just when shit got real.

"Please explain to this little girl that I will lay her body six feet under while she's still breathing then kill the rest of her family," Milagros exposed while handing me the phone.

I spat an insult and threat at that ho' before I hung up. Ty's days were now definitely numbered before Milagros beat that ass. I was going to hold her off of Ty until she had the babies. I did have a heart, but I need to keep my focus straight.

Ever since hooking up with Milagros I had been thrown into a different league. When baby said she was a boss, she was most certainly that! She was showing me things I had never seen before, taking me places I had never been and doing shit I had never done before. Hell, I was just like McDonald's. I was loving it!

Just her house alone made me wonder why I wasn't living like her. Yes, I had long money but I knew nothing about property. She had to school me on that shit.

Milagros was the truth for real. She had a nigga wide open and I wasn't about to let her go. I was already a leader, but she was grooming me to be a real boss.

The first thing she did was take me to her hometown of Rio de Janeiro. It was fucking beautiful! I wasn't even stunting the women there because Milagros was all that I needed and then some.

The night we got back to town, we left the airport in separate cars because she had a meeting. By the time I handled my business, she was calling me to come over.

I showed up at her house and she showed out for a real nigga. Her ass answered the door butt ass naked with a pair of six-inch stiletto red bottom heels on. My shit was on brick right away.

She pulled me into the house and immediately dropped to her knees. She had my dick in her mouth in less than two seconds and I was in Heaven. I was receiving some of the best head I had ever had in my life. She slurped and slobbed on my knob for all of five minutes before my toes were curling and I was screaming like a little bitch. She swallowed all my babies and kept going. She had my shit right back on hard in no time.

I pulled her up and stuck my tongue so far down her throat that I swear I felt her tonsils. I savored her kiss even though she had just ingested my nut juice. I was all into the kiss when she broke away from me.

"I have so much more in store for you Amon. Come. Follow me so I can show you how a real queen does for her king."

I wasted no time following right behind the nice, plump, fat ass that was in front of me. We went up the stairs and all the way to the last room on the second floor. When I walked in, I was impressed. The room was decked out in black and royal purple. There was something that looked like a swing in one corner with a metal rod dead in the middle of the room. My eyes bulged out my head as I watched Milagros approach the pole.

"Grab that chair over in the corner and come here Amon. Watch how a queen performs for her king."

I did as I was told and quickly snatched up the chair so I could enjoy the show. Milagros climbed the pole like a pro and did a trick with her legs before landing in a split in front of me. I swear she had a nigga mesmerized.

She got up real slow and gripped pole again as she bent over and made it clap for me. I pulled the knot of money I had out of my pocket and started making it rain on Milagros. She kept twirling around the pole and showing out. By the time she was done, she had worked up a sweat so she asked me to follow her to the bathroom. Once inside I noticed how huge it was. She was doing things on a much bigger scale than I was. Shit, I was trying to get like her.

I watched her as she started the shower and removed her stilettos. I noticed the shower had a bar overhead where the water came raining down and on either side of the wall there were streams of water shooting out at high pressure. She motioned for me to join her and I wasted no time stripping down to my birthday suit.

I caught the expression on her face and I knew that she was surprised at the sight of my package. I guess she thought that because I was a young buck I had a young dick. Nah. I was about to show her cougar ass something.

I stepped into the shower and eased right behind Milagros. She leaned back and laid her head on my shoulder. I couldn't resist planting light kisses on her neck. She moaned like she was in need and I was about to give her everything she wanted. I pushed her forward, grabbed her by her neck and smacked her on her wet ass. All she did was moan some more and clutch her ankles. That was my cue to tear that ass up.

I slid into her wet slit with no mercy. I heard Milagros gasp then squeal in pleasure. I gripped her hips and pumped into her forcefully. I wasn't showing any pity on that ass. I dug deep in her guts as she moaned and groaned. We stayed in the shower until the water went cold and even then I was still tearing that ass up.

I cut the shower off and pulled out of her. I picked her up and carried her to the king sized bed before I tossed her down. Wet and everything, Milagros was sexy as fuck! She crawled over to the edge of the bed and took my wood into her mouth once more.

I almost lost myself in another head session before I pulled back. I pushed her onto the bed and took hold of her ankles. I knelt down, now it my turn to display my cunnilingus skills. I slurped and sucked on her pussy like I was dehydrated and her juices were the only thing could quench my thirst.

All of a sudden, Milagros began squirming and calling out my name like I was God himself.

"Amon! Amonnnnn! Aaaaaaaaammmmmmooooooonnnnn! Oh... My... Godddddd!"

"Yeah baby say that shit. This my pussy now?" I asked her.

"Yes! Oh God yes! Yes my muthafuckin' king!"

"King?" Yeah I liked the sound of that shit, especially when it rolled off her lips.

I stroked the hell outta Milagros as she screamed out in pleasure and pain. Then the tables turned. She had me hollering a few times when she got on top of me and started riding me. Her pussy was definitely A-1.

"I could get used to this shit here." I thought silently.

Once we were both spent, we lay in the aftermath of our bliss. As I was placing kisses on her face and neck, Milagros checked her cell. Seconds later she spoke.

"I hate to ruin the mood my king but we have a situation we need to handle."

What is it my queen?"

"Your little girlfriend Ty and her baby daddy Aiden. I already want to show her how I handle shit and her little boyfriend has been extra busy lately."

Now she had my full attention.

"What do you mean?"

"Well the word is that he's been asking around for you or where to find you. Apparently he feels like you two have some unfinished business to settle when it comes to that hoodrat."

"Say no more. I'll handle it in the morning."

"I thought you would say that so I took the liberty of putting things in motion already. It will be handled tonight. Now all you have to worry about is scratching this itch that I have."

I prayed she wasn't speaking of killing Ty. I couldn't live with that shit on my conscience. I played it down and went along with her spill.

"Damn baby I like how you move. About that itch though... I can scratch it all night if you want me to."

"How about forever?"

With that said I got up and pressed my body to hers as I kissed her deeply. She ain't said nothing but a word. If forever was what she wanted then forever is what she would get...

Ty'Keisha

Another couple of weeks had passed and I found out that Amon had been kicking it strong with the Milagros bitch. I was doing everything in my power to find out where either of them rested their heads. I knew that they still kept separate domains, so I didn't think their bond was that damn strong.

"Did you find out where that nigga lives yet?" I yelled at Aiden as I rubbed my oversized belly. The twins were quickly growing and my due date was nearing.

"Let me handle that shit baby," Aiden urged as he picked up my foot to rub it. "Just relax. I got a couple of leads that I'm gonna check out tonight."

"I know me too," I admitted. "La'Karata told me that they were out of the damn country. If they are still gone this would be the perfect time to creep up in they shit and set some traps."

"No worries Ty'Keisha," Aiden promised. "I will have them both bleeding and breathless by the end of this week."

My mind wanted to believe the shit, but my gut told me a completely different story. I listened to my gut.

Waiting for Aiden to leave the room, I snatched up my cell and dialed La'Karata. I wanted to know if she was able to steal the poison from the hospital. I needed that shit for what I had planned for Milagros. I wanted her and everyone close to her dead!

"Yeah, I got that shit!" La'Karata barked. "Do you got them ends?"

"I got a 'G'," I shot back as I rubbed my hands together while holding the phone between my cheek and shoulder. "Meet me at the spot over on the South Side."

"Thirty minutes," she blurted out before hanging up.

"I'll be there."

Although I didn't trust La'Karata, I needed her. I was far from dumb though. I kept records of all of our dealings. If I was going down for some shit, so the fuck was she!

"Let me go baby," Aiden suggested.

"I need to handle this shit. If she sees you that bitch might think we gonna jump her or some shit. You know that ho' paranoid."

"I'm going!"

"What?"

"Just what the hell I said! If you trippin' about me riding with you, I can drive my own car. Either way, I'm going."

"Why we always gotta argue Aiden?"

"This right here aint a damn argument. I spoke my peace now just roll with the shit, baby, please."

Once I saw that I wasn't about to win, I gave in and agreed to him driving his own whip. I was too tired to fuss and my stomach was starting to cramp.

"Are you alright?" Aiden questioned as he watched me clutch my stomach. "Just call that bitch back and tell her that we'll catch up with her later."

"No, this may be my only chance to get back at the bitch! She don' threatened us and I know she's just waiting to catch us slipping. We need to get her ass first!"

"Well, come the hell on and then I'm taking you to the hospital to get checked out. You have to think about the twins too Ty'Keisha!"

"No, you can come with me, but I'm driving!" I insisted. "If I'm still hurting after the pickup, then we can go to the hospital, okay?"

"Cool," Aiden agreed. "You need to go though, because this is too early for you to go in labor and shit."

Taking swift steps, I made my way to the car with my baby daddy on my neck. I swear that man was too much.

"Don't be driving all crazy and shit either Ty'Keisha," Aiden warned. "I'm strapped and we don't need a fucking interview."

Aiden slowly drew his shiny chrome handgun and cocked it back to release one into the chamber. An anxious rush ran through my body as I watched him prepare himself for battle.

"We're just going to pick something up Aiden," I laughed. "Why are you actin' so damn paranoid?"

"You think I trust that La'Karata chick?" he clowned. "That bitch was fucking the Amon nigga too!"

Aiden shook his head in disgust. I knew what he was thinking, but I didn't have time to entertain the shit at the moment.

"There she go right there," I whispered aloud as I turned around and pulled up next to her. I was shocked as shit to see her belly sticking out. Yeah the ho' was pregnant but I didn't have time to be all up in her business.

"Yo"

"Damn, don't be sneakin' up on me and shit Ty!"

"Why you so jumpy?"

"Bitch just give me the money and take yo shit," she smirked while handing me a small paper bag.

We did the exchange and then hurried to veer back off into traffic. Soon as we did, Aiden sat straight up and began barking directions.

"Turn left at the corner!"

I obeyed and picked up the pace a bit.

"Turn left again at the stop sign."

After I swung a left I heard the first gun shot. Aiden wasted no time returning fire.

"Pow, bang, pow."

I could hear at least two different sounds, alerting me there were two shooters. They were right on us. I couldn't shake them.

"I'm trying to get them..."

"What?"

Turning to Aiden, I saw that he was hit and slowly slumping down into the seat. I tried my hardest not to panic, but once my stomach began cramping I couldn't help it.

"I gotta make it to get some help," I thought out loud just as I felt something hot pierce me in the shoulder. The next one hit me in the arm.

"No, no, no," I cried. "I gotta make it to the hospital! Please Lord let me make it!"

Just as I turned onto the street that the medical facility was located, I felt a bullet hit the right side of my neck. I could see the blood spew onto the window. Taking my left hand, I held on to my throat to stop it from leaking.

"Please help me!" I gasped as I pulled up to the emergency entrance and rolled out of my car. "My babies save my babies."

All I remembered before blacking out was a baby crying...

Amon Rivers

Milagros got a call around four in the morning and quickly woke me up. She shoved the cell in my face and told me that it was someone for me. I grabbed the phone and barked into it.

"Yeah who is this?"

"Is this a Mister Amon Rivers?"

"Yeah now what do you want at this ungodly hour?"

"I am so sorry for disturbing you this early. My name is Dr. Ayar and I work in the emergency department at Mercy Hospital. A young woman by the name of Ty'Keisha Johnson listed you as her next of kin."

"Hold up, what? Next of kin? For what though? What happened?"

"Well there was an accident and seems as though she was a victim of a shooting. She arrived at the hospital several hours ago bleeding profusely from a gunshot wound to the neck. She was also pregnant and said that you were the father. We took her into surgery and had her stable for a little while but right before she crashed, she gave a nurse your number and told the nurse to contact the father of her twins. I need you to come to the hospital right away sir."

"Alright I'm on my way!" I yelled into the phone before hanging up.

I jumped out of the bed in a panic to find my clothes. As I was slipping on my jogging pants, I noticed that Milagros was still sitting in the bed. I looked at her and saw that she had a funny smirk on her face.

"You still care about the little bitch don't you?"

"Nah it ain't that, but I do care about those babies though because they're innocent in all this."

"Man fuck them babies Amon!"

My heart went out to Ty because I truly loved her. I never wished death on her or those kids. She was my first real girlfriend...

Suddenly I felt my tear duct fill. I had to shit my thoughts and think of some bullshit excuse. I couldn't believe the stupid shit I came up with.

"Think about it Milly. We can use them to our advantage. They don't know who their parents are right now. We can raise them as our own and train them as we see fit."

"How do you figure that will work Amon? I'm real curious as to what you think will happen."

"Ok check this out. Remember how I told you when we first started this shit that we would need to put two people in place for something big but we would need time to mold them. I said two younger people would be needed. They would both need to be parentless and impressionable. What better than two kids, two babies at that, with no mother? This is what we need."

"I remember you mentioning it briefly but who said I wanted to be anyone's mother?"

"Don't look at it that way. Look at it as though you're being their mentor. Someone they can look up to and would never question your word."

"Hmmmm. That could work. I'll tell you this now though Amon, I will not be disrespected. One time and I'll get rid of them myself. Understood?"

"Understood my queen. Now let's go get these babies." I replied hoping that she was over exaggerating when she said 'get rid of them'.

Milagros bought it all and rushed to get dressed herself as I finished getting ready. We were out the door and headed towards the expressway in no time.

We arrived at Mercy Hospital approximately forty minutes later. We went straight to the front desk and had them call for Dr. Ayar.

"Dr. Ayar will be with you momentarily." She informed with a smile.

Milagros and I took a seat in the waiting area. While we were talking, a doctor called my name.

"Mister Amon Rivers?"

"Yes sir, Dr. Ayar?"

"Yes. If you'll just follow me. We can walk and talk if you don't mind."

"Sure no problem."

"Ok Mr. Rivers. As I told you over the phone, Ms. Johnson named you the father to her twin girls. The babies are in the nursery as of right now. Ms. Johnson also had a companion with her who died. A Mr. Aiden Thomas. Do you know him?"

"I just know that's who she started dating after we split. Can you take me to see my babies?"

I heard Milagros suck her teeth but I gave her a look that told her to calm that shit down. Last thing I needed was for her to stray from the plan. If I was king then her ass had better learn to trust me and whatever I did; with no fucking questions.

I followed behind the doctor as he led us to the nursery. When we arrived at the end of the hall, we stopped in front of a big glass window. He tapped twice on it and held up two fingers. I didn't know what that meant until I saw two nurses wheeling two baby bassinets to the window. I looked down at these two little girls and instantly fell in love. I made sure to keep calm so that Milagros wouldn't see how I was feeling.

Even though I knew they weren't mine, I felt some type of connection to them. I guess it was because I actually loved Ty once upon a time. It made me feel that same love towards her daughters.

Glancing over at Milagros, I noticed a smile spread across her face. Thing was, I couldn't tell if it was genuine or not...

"Doc can I hold my daughters?"

"Sure you can. Follow me."

The doctor led us inside the nursery to a sitting area. The girls were brought to us and I was handed one baby while Milagros was handed the other. I stared at the sleeping baby that I held but Milagros had the baby that was wide awake. We switched so I could interact with the feisty one.

"Ahem. My name is Nurse Jean and I was wondering if you would be up to filling out the girls' birth certificates?" she interrupted.

"Of course I would. Can you give us a few minutes to think it over? I was totally unprepared for this because their mother said we had about another month to go before they were born."

"Sure thing. Just let me know when you're ready."

The nurse walked away and I looked at Milagros. She had a blank expression on her face because she was just as lost as I was.

"Two girls."

What could we possibly name them? We sat deep in thought for a moment before my eyes lit up. Milagros looked at me with a surprised expression before saying anything.

"You look like a light bulb went off in your head my love."

"It did. I know what to name them."

"Enlighten me."

"Adora Reyna and Soledad Amada."

"Why those names?"

"Look at how they are now. I have one sleeping, quiet baby. She seems like she may be the calmer of the two and like the solitude she may get. Adora for the one you're holding because she looks like she's going to want attention a lot; to be adored by someone. I couldn't think of anything better for them."

"Then that's what their names will be. Excuse me, Nurse Jean?" Milagros called out.

"Yes ma'am."

"We've decided on names for the girls. The one Amon is holding will be Soledad Amada and the one I'm holding will be Adora Reyna."

"Awesome! Let me get you the paperwork you will need to fill out."

Nurse Jean rushed away to get the paperwork and I just looked at Milagros. She was such an amazing woman. To take these little girls into our lives was a huge thing. I just prayed that in time she would learn to love them the way I was starting to. I needed her to make things work.

We placed the girls back into their bassinets that another nurse had wheeled over for us. We were going to be parents. With my woman and two beautiful little girls, nothing could stop us.

Milagros waited patiently while I filled out the proper documents for the girls. They informed me that I could pick them up the following day.

We left the hospital hand in hand on the way to our car. I had to know how my queen was feeling so I decided to pick her brain.

"I just want to know, how do you feel about all of this Milagros?"

"I feel fine about it I guess. At first, I was apprehensive but when I saw you with them I just couldn't say no. They are beautiful and even though they aren't yours, I will still help you raise them like they are. You have nothing to worry about mi amor."

"That's all I needed to hear from you. You are something special you know that woman?"

"And so are you. That is why I chose you to be my king. With us together, we are unstoppable."

I let her words sink in and tried my best to believe them as I cranked up the car and headed out of the parking garage. 'Unstoppable', I sure did like the sound of that.

<u>Milagros</u>

Yes, every 'Street Queen' needed her 'Street King' and Amon Rivers was my number one candidate. He currently held hood status and that was a plus for me because I already had the corporate game on lock.

Although I had prominent ties in the hood, very few trusted me because of my wealth and power. Thing was, I was just as down as the next baller chick only I had the backing of an empire.

Amon's only flaw was the bitch Ty'Keisha he was fooling with. When I had her and her dude taken out I thought that was the end of the trick. Oh, how wrong I was about that shit.

I couldn't believe that her twins survived the shooting! That was my fucking Karma though. I myself couldn't have kids because of an accident that happened when I was just a teenager. Now there I was about to be forced to be a parent to two girls that I wanted nothing to do with. Hell, I had their fucking mother killed and I knew if that ever got out the tables could surely turn.

I knew it was the perfect time to tell Amon about me not being able to conceive, but right then I felt that I had too much to lose. I had already invested too much into our relationship.

Instead of stirring shit up, I decided to go with the flow and see how things turned out.

"We have a lot of shit to do before we bring the girls home," Amon blurted out then looked over at me.

"What?"

"Where is home? You stayin' with me or I'm stayin' with you?"

Feeling the need to be in control of the entire situation, I suggested that they all move in with me. It was a big step, but I needed to ensure the success of what we were trying to accomplish. Plus, I wanted to keep Amon close.

"First thing you need to do is hire a nanny," I smirked. "I ain't with 2am feedings and shitty diapers. Now when they're walking and talking I'm cool, but until then we're going to need a whole lot of help."

"Cool, I'll call a few agencies and check into it," Amon offered.

"No, no, no," I snapped and rolled my eyes. "I will call one of my relatives and have them do it. I don't want any outsiders in my home... I mean our home."

Amon hit me with an unsettling expression that I couldn't read. When I questioned him about it, he asked once again how I was feeling about keeping the twins. It was yet another chance to back out of the situation, but I couldn't. I couldn't risk messing up my master plan.

"Let's just call up a decorator and have them convert one of the extra rooms into a nursery so the girls have somewhere to sleep. As far as shopping for clothes and food, I'll let you handle that. I need to rest up before tomorrow. This is going to be a job."

Amon stayed silent as if he was in deep thought. I had no idea what he was thinking, but the way he was frowned up prevented me from prying.

"I'm gonna drop you off at the house. I know you wanna hop in ya own ride. I'm gonna run and take care of the shit I need to do." He explained as we arrived in my neighborhood. "You think you can take care of doing the room though? I'll do everything else."

"Of course," I gritted through a smile.

"Thanks Milly," he replied with a huge grin that melted my heart.

Yes, I truly loved Amon but the shit he had with him was weighing my patience. I just prayed that I didn't have to lighten the load anytime soon...

"Call me if you need me baby."

"Alright King," I smiled stroking his ego. "You can just drop me in the front. I need to talk to Medina the housekeeper to have her to help me with some things."

Stealing a little kiss before I got out, I pranced my ass in the house knowing good and well that I wasn't about to do shit. I planned on having Medina and the rest of my staff do everything. I was about to hop in my ride and go get a manicure and pedicure.

"Ring, ring"

"Who the hell is this?" I huffed as I connected the call.

"Milagros this is La'Karata and I just wanted to call you and tell you that I know you had Lamar and his brother kill Ty'Keisha. You think these streets don't talk. It's only a matter of time before Amon finds out you had her taken out."

"Bitch please! Amon didn't give a damn about that hood rat and he damn sure don't give a rat's ass about you! So, what the hell are you doing tying up my line with some bullshit?"

"I see how you danced all around the subject pertaining to you killing Ty'Keisha, but we gonna see." La'Karata spat. "See the difference is, the streets loved Ty and you, well, you're just a fuckin' outsider that's about to meet her maker."

"Are these threats you're shooting at me?"

"I don't have to touch you bitch!" she came sideways. "There's a list of motherfuckers dying to touch your foreign ass. That's okay. Tell your family they are about to receive a wooden box FedEx, compliments of the streets of Chicago."

"Bitch I run this shit!" I yelled becoming upset. "I run shit on a level you know nothing about."

"Okay, I'll give you that, but the level these niggas are on that are after yo ass is one you've never reached... guaranteed!"

"I will dead you, Lamar and his gay ass brother if I hear one hum of my name in the streets behind Ty'Keisha's murder... guaranteed!"

I hung up on her and had my number changed immediately. I called Amon and gave him the new one. Of course he questioned me, but I gave him some hurried excuse that he bought as always. Yes, I just had it like that...

Amon Rivers

It seemed like shit was getting hectic around the hood but everything was all good in my home. After I dropped Milagros off at the house, I made my way to a few of my spots to check up on everything.

Everybody was talking about what happened to Ty. Even a few people came and asked me if I knew what happened with her twins. I just kept telling everybody that I didn't know. I didn't need any of their nosy asses in my business. They would all know in due time…

I was chilling in front of one of my spots talking to DJ when La'Karata rolled up on me. I swear that bitch was bugging! She was in true hood rat fashion complete with pajamas and a headscarf. I shook my head at her appearance. She looked like she had gained weight but she was wearing it well.

"Damn Amon, I see you on some other shit. I know it was yo bitch that killed my girl!" La'Karata shouted loudly for everyone around to hear.

I was pissed and wanted to knock her head off her shoulders but I kept my cool. I walked around her car and snatched her ass by her arm.

"Oh, so now that's ya girl?" I smirked.

"Amon, let me the fuck go! You're hurting me."

"Oh trust me bitch, I ain't hurt you yet."

"That's what we do now Amon. So you gone have someone kill me too?"

"What the fuck are you talking about? I ain't kill no fucking body! Yo ass is just tripping cuz I don't fuck with you no more."

"Yeah ok Amon. You ain't got no choice but to fuck with me now because in about six months we'll be parents."

"Oh hell naw! I don't need this shit right now. I already had one bitch try to pin kids on me, and now you pulling that bullshit. Fuck outta here!"

KING OF CHICAGO

"You ain't gotta believe me now but when that DNA comes back saying 99.99% that you are the father then you will."

"Man La, I don't need this shit so holla at me when you drop. Until then we ain't got shit to say to each other and kill that fucking noise about my girl having Ty killed. That Aiden nigga she was with was grimy as fuck. You know the streets talk so ask about him. He wasn't as square as y'all thought he was."

La'Karata sucked her teeth at me before turning to leave. "Another baby my ass! I'll be damned."

Now as far as getting rid of that bitch, it needed to happen ASAP. I would just have to add that to my list of shit to do.

After saying my goodbyes to DJ and the rest of the crew, I headed out. I pulled up to North Riverside Mall right off Cermak Road so I could go shopping for my girls.

"My girls" Damn I was a father. I was going to enjoy spoiling Soledad and Adora. I knew that I'd have to do something huge for Milagros too because she was going along with my wishes but I could tell she didn't like it.

I hit Children's Place, Baby Gap and even Build-A-Bear for the girls. I made a special stop at Zale's to grab Milagros something to show my appreciation. I needed her to stick to the plan I had brewing in my head. I knew once I explained all the specifics that she would be on board.

In the middle of my shopping spree, I got a phone call about some shit at one of my houses. I wrapped everything up and headed back out west.

"I see muthafuckas thought I was playing with them." Well, they were about to learn why Twan handed things over to me and why Milagros chose me.

I sped down the 290 to get there faster. When I got off and hit the hood, I pulled up to our spot on Kimball Avenue. DJ immediately greeted me. No words were exchanged as we headed inside. Right before we entered the house DJ stopped me.

"Hey Cuz I gotta let you know something before we go in here."

"Well what's up?"

"The nigga who popped off and pulled some bullshit, it's our cousin."

"Our cousin who?"

"Dub."

I just shook my head. Dub, or Colay as we knew him, was my cousin on my mama's side. Me and DJ really didn't like his little ass but because he was family we put him on. Now I had to fuck up my own damn blood. Ain't this some shit?

I walked inside and saw that Dub was already tied up with a gag in his mouth. There was plastic spread on the floor under him because it might get messy. I was definitely gonna fuck this little nigga up but I wouldn't kill him. I would just cut his ass off. I walked up on him.

WHACK!

"Nobody steals from me and gets away with it. What you thought you was exempt from some shit cuz we family? Nah Cuz, you already know how I get down."

I spat on the floor after working my cousin over. He was a little goofy ass nigga and I felt sorry for him because his mama was a crackhead. That was the only reason why I decided to put him on so he wouldn't be out in the streets running with another nigga's crew who didn't give a fuck about him. 'So much for my fucking hospitality.' After all the shit I did for his little ungrateful ass he felt the need to steal from me. I couldn't let that shit fly and decided to make an example of him to the rest of the niggas I rolled with.

"Let this be a lesson to all you lil niggas that's in my camp. If I'll fuck my blood up for stealing from me then what you think I'll do to one of y'all?"

I stared at each man I had in attendance. I had everyone from my top lieutenants to my street runners and corner boys. I wanted each one of them to know that I didn't take any shorts or losses.

That was not how I became respected in the hood. I ran my shit the same way those Wall Street niggas ran a Fortune 500 company. I needed my shit airtight at all times. I had no room for mistakes whatsoever.

Being cautious is what kept me in the game for so long. If there was a glitch in my system, then I fixed it. It was just that simple. Smart niggas feared me and knew to keep my name out of their mouth. Those who chose to step out of the circle and run their mouths got dealt with. It was as simple as that...

That type of loyalty and respect couldn't be bought it had to be earned. Many a nigga had tried to knock me off my throne but there was only one King of Chicago and that was I, Amon Rivers.

Now I had to figure out what that bitch ass nigga Colay did with my bread. Supposedly he stole somewhere near half a million from me. Maybe I could ask his baby mama. She was always cool people with me and I really didn't want to involve her but for my money to be found I needed to.

I told DJ what to do as I hopped in my car to head to Marina's house. It was going to be a long ass night for me. I knew that whenever I made it home I would have to do some serious ass kissing.

I pulled up in front of Marina and Colay's house moments later. I saw that all the lights were out but I figured it was because it was almost 10PM. I noticed their nosy ass neighbor, Ms. Jenkins, was sitting on her porch eyeballing me but I paid her no mind.

I rang the doorbell and waited. After about a minute or so I didn't hear anything so I started to knock. Still no answer. I started beating on the door getting agitated when Ms. Jenkins finally got my attention.

"Young man! Ain't no sense in beating on that door because ain't nobody there."

"What you mean ain't nobody there?"

"That young lady with all them kids left earlier this month. Ain't no telling where she went but I know she finally left that no good man that she was with."

"What the fuck? Do you have a number on her?"

"No young man I don't, but she did say she was going somewhere far away from here and him and that she would never come back."

"Ok Ms. Jenkins, thanks so much for that info. I appreciate it."

"No problem young man."

I hopped back in my car pissed off like hell. First Colay was stealing from me and now Marina was gone. Either he was going to cough up my money or his baby mama would find out about me. I decided to call it a night after that shit. Before I did, I hit DJ up and told him to keep an eye on Colay so we wouldn't lose track of his ass. I wasn't about to let that shit happen.

I sped down the 290 expressway to go home. I hoped that Milagros had taken care of the nursery for the girls as I wanted and needed her to. To reward her, I was going to make my woman feel very good because the following day we would be bringing the girls home. I knew that once they got there we wouldn't have too many nights alone.

I pulled up in front of the house and turned my car off. I hoped that once I got inside Milagros was asleep. It would make my night easier because my day had been quite eventful. I let myself in the front door and locked it behind me.

I made my way up the stairs and towards the master bedroom. On my way down the hallway I noticed one of the other bedroom doors open. I stepped in the doorway and was at a loss for words. Everything was ready for the girls and my woman had done her thing. There were twin cribs and dressers on opposite sides of the room. There was also two playpens, a rocking chair and all types of girly stuff decorating the room.

Both girls' names were spelled across the walls above their cribs and everything was pink, white and purple. It was truly a room fit for two princesses. I would definitely be thanking my woman for all this. I made my way to our bedroom to start my freak session.

As soon as I entered the room I was taken aback. Milagros was sitting in the king-sized high back chair I sat in when she gave me a show our first night together. She was stark naked and playing with her clean shaven pussy. I was immediately turned on. A nigga could get used to coming home to that shit.

Initially I was prepared to discuss business first and then get down to the pleasure part, but after that view, I pushed it to the back of my mind.

Quickly stripping out of my clothes, I crawled on my hands and knees to Milagros' feet. I wasted no time burying my face into her sweet spot. Amidst her moans I reached up and tweaked her nipples. She let out a loud growl.

I continued feasting on her kitty until I felt her legs start to shake. I locked my arms around her thighs and held on tight as she started to buck. I kept swirling my tongue around in her juice box until her squirming stopped. I slurped up the last remaining drops of her juices before I released her.

I looked up at her to see that she was completely satisfied. The expression on her face told it all.

Rising to my feet with my erect pole staring her in the face, I gestured her to get her slob on. She wasted no time in taking me into her mouth. I moaned with pleasure and thrust my hands into her hair.

She let me pump in and out her mouth with no mercy as I felt my nut building up. In one swoop she deep throated me and cupped my balls at the same time. I busted quickly down into her oral cavity. Now I was the one who was wearing the satisfied look.

We both went to lay down in the bed and I pulled Milagros as close to me as I could. As I went to kiss her forehead she spoke.

"Amon I can't say that I'm completely happy with the decision you've made concerning Ty's daughters but I will stand behind you 100% on it. I know that if you're doing this now then there has to be some kind of plan as to why. I will follow your lead baby."

"Thank you so much baby. Trust me everything will be revealed soon, I promise you. There is definitely a reason for me doing this." I replied.

"Well, speaking of reasons for doing things. I need to fix this little La'Karata bitch. She called me today popping shit about how she knows I had something to do with Ty being killed."

"It's funny you say that babe because I saw her today and she was popping the same shit at me about you killing Ty. I wondered why. Anyway, I had to tell her lil ass that she don't know shit and warned her not to become a problem for us. So what do you suggest we do about her?"

Instantly thinking back to Ty's murder, I wondered if Milagros had it done. I didn't want to ask because I didn't want to hear the answer. I knew that if she revealed that she did indeed have her killed, I would flip.

"She gotta go. Last thing I need is for anybody actually believing her and coming for us. We can't afford that shit with the girls coming home. I need to make sure we all stay safe." She stated sounding sincere.

SHELLI MARIE & MARINA J

"Bam, she's admitting that she didn't do," I tried to convince myself silently.

I erased my ill thoughts and got close to my woman.

"True that. Man I love you for how you always think ahead. You got me baby."

"You know I do," Milagros chuckled.

"Let's talk about that tomorrow some time. Tonight I gotta please my woman."

"Now I love the sound of that baby."

I dove under the blanket and orally pleased Milagros for another round. Her moans of pleasure turned me on and my dick was rock hard once again. I stopped my oral assault and jumped up to thrust my dick into her. She gasped upon my entry. I went to work on her tight snatch as she groaned in pleasure. I kept digging deeper and deeper into her as she called out my name. We both climaxed moments later.

Basking in the afterglow of our lovemaking, we both drifted off to sleep. *Tomorrow our lives would change forever...*

PART THREE
THE LEGEND

Milagros

8 YEARS LATER...

"Amon, when are you gonna be home?" I questioned after finally reaching him. I had already called him over a dozen times just to get his voicemail.

Although business was booming, my love life was pure shit. If Amon wasn't running to the girls every five minutes, he was in the streets getting money. I couldn't understand the shit because that was what we had workers for.

No matter how much money we made, Amon wouldn't stay out off the block. For some reason he felt his presence was needed to ensure a proper flow. That was that bullshit...

"I'll be there within the hour," he huffed as if my complaining was getting on his nerves. "Are the girls home from school?"

That was all he ever talked about. I swear he told me that he just wanted to get the twins and raise them to work for us, but it wasn't like that. The bond that they were developing was tight and not even I could loosen it...

"Yes, they are in the study doing their homework."

"Did they get something to eat or do I need to bring them something?"

"Aint that a bitch?" I thought to myself.

I frowned up, held the phone from my ear and gave it a mean mug as if Amon could see me. He had a lot of nerve. He didn't even ask if I was hungry or if I ate!

"Yes, you know that's the first thing they did!" I gritted through my teeth.

"Okay, I'll be there," he stated before hanging up. Hell, I didn't even get a chance to say goodbye!

"Milly, where's my dad?" Adora questioned rushing into my bedroom. "I need him to sign some papers for me."

"Bring them here. I can do it for you." I offered only for her to give me a fucked up look.

"It's okay. I'll wait for my dad," she smiled crookedly as she turned around and stepped out of the room.

I could hear Soledad try and scold her twin sister for not allowing me to sign the papers for her. She instructed her to be good and obey. I knew better to think Adora would listen.

The twins were now in grade school. The older they got, not only did they take to Amon; they also began to favor him. I had been questioning him about it for years, but he swore to me that there was no way that they could be.

"I know the truth will come to the light!" I thought silently as I searched for something to occupy my time.

After debating with myself for the next five minutes, I decided to clean my closet out, which took over an hour. That's when Amon came home.

He didn't even come and check on me. He went straight to the twins and asked if they wanted to go get some ice cream.

"Milly, I'm about to take the girls out to Baskin and Robbins. We'll be back." Amon shouted up the stairs.

"No, I don't want any," I mumbled silently becoming more upset.

I didn't even entertain him with a response. Instead, I sucked my teeth and got some clothes on. I needed a stress reliever and since I wasn't getting any dick, I thought I'd take myself out for a drink or two.

I hurried to get dressed before Amon came home. I definitely didn't need him questioning me.

Rushing to hop in the car, I turned the volume up on the radio and raced off towards the west side. I knew the perfect little spot to hit...

****

It was nearly three in the morning when I finally made it home. I didn't purposely stay out all night. It was just that I had ran into some old friends and wound up closing the damn club. My man wasn't too happy with me when I got there.

"Where the hell have you been?" Amon questioned me as I staggered my drunk ass into the bedroom.

"Out drinking," I admitted without a lick of shame. "I'm grown and was stayin' in my own lane. You don't have a problem with that do you?"

Now Amon was acting a little beside himself and I was in no mood to argue so I didn't push the issue. Luckily he didn't either. He had something else on his mind.

"Look, the twins have a doctor's appointment in the morning and I can't take them because of that meeting I have up north."

"So, what are you saying?"

"Can you take them or naw?" Amon huffed hesitantly.

Suddenly a bright idea came in my mind.

"Sure, I'll take them," I replied as I undressed and headed to the shower.

"What?"

"What?"

"Nothing, I just can't believe you said yes without me havin' to sweat you."

"Sweat me?" I snapped then quickly calmed down remembering my ulterior motive.

Amon stomped off. I knew I touched a nerve, but I made that shit up to him as soon as I got myself cleaned up. I had him snoring and slobbering within the next hour. Shit, I was right behind him...

****

"Baby, wake up!" Amon shouted out making me damn near jump out of my skin to check the time. "It's seven and the twin's appointment is at eight!"

I began getting ready and asked Amon to make sure the girls were doing the same before he left out the door. I couldn't understand why he woke me up at the last minute instead of when he got his monkey ass up. Ugh, I swear he got on my nerves at times and if these test results proved that he was indeed the twins father we were about to have some serious problems...

"Come on Soledad and Adora!" I shouted from the open door. "We gotta go!"

They both ran right by me, stepping on my new shoes and damn near knocking me over. I wanted to snatch them up and beat both of them!

"Get in and buckle up," I instructed as I started the car and turned up the music to drown out Adora mumbling under her breath.

I glanced back in the mirror only to see them both frowning up. I couldn't get why they saw me as the enemy. Even though I didn't spend time with them, I always made sure they had everything they needed.

"Oh well, I'm not gonna try my best not to trip until I know for sure that they aren't Amon's!" I plotted silently. "He better pray to God that they aren't!"

Several minutes later, we arrived at the clinic. "Come on girls we're here."

"We're coming," Adora gritted as she nudged her twin sister in the arm.

"Stop it!" Soledad whispered with a frown then yelled out. "We're coming."

When we walked in, I told the girls to go and take a seat in the waiting area. I needed to go and set up the test without them knowing anything about it. That was all I needed was for them to go running to 'daddy' and tell on a bitch...

"Ma'am," I smiled. "I also need some other tests done while we're here.

Once I finished explaining what I wanted, she turned her face up and told me that she couldn't do it without their father's written consent.

"I can sign the papers," I whispered as I slid her five crisp one hundred dollar bills.

She snatched them up and handed me the necessary documents to fill out.

"I'll need a sample from him as well.

"Will this do?" I questioned as I retrieved the Ziploc baggie from my jacket pocket.

The plastic sack contained Amon's toothbrush. That was the only thing I could think to grab…

"We'll have the results back to you next week." She spoke on the low with a wink.

I smiled and made sure she sent them directly to me. I had a private post office box and email address that Amon knew nothing about. I knew that they would come in handy one day…

Amon Rivers

I could not believe that eight years had passed. After traveling down to North Carolina and fixing that situation with Colay, life was good. I was glad that Marina had nothing to do with it because I had always liked her. I really didn't want to harm her or her kids.

It seemed like all of our problems had disappeared at once too. La'Karata had even made herself invisible.

I was a doting father to Soledad and Adora. I knew they weren't biologically mine but we had built an amazing bond. I knew that they didn't like Milagros for whatever reason and I had to admit that lately even our relationship was strained.

Don't get me wrong, I loved Milagros for everything she gave me, how she upgraded my status and put me where I was at today. I truly was the *King of Chicago*.

I ran everything from north to south and east to west. My reach was impressive and my money was extra-long. I was winning in every department except my love life.

When I had to go down to North Carolina, I ended up bringing a chick named Tina back with me. At first, it wasn't on any get together type of shit because I had Milagros. Tina was a certified hacker and genius so we had some things in common. The more time I spent with her, the more I started to fall in love with her mind.

Tina reminded me a whole lot of Ty. She was headstrong and had that hood swag about her which was sexy as hell.

I was now stuck between two women when it came to my heart. I felt like I was obligated to stay with Milagros but Tina was starting to sway that decision.

I shook that whole thing from my mind as I focused on the twins. Their upbringing was my pride and joy.

In the beginning, my initial reason for taking the girls after Ty died was because I honestly felt obligated. Then I grew to really love those little girls and had a change of heart about the situation.

It was funny though. The older Soledad and Adora got, the more they started to favor me. That was when Milagros started getting in my ass about them really being mine. Every time I turned around she was bumping her gums about a damn DNA test but I wasn't trying to hear it. I knew they weren't mine and Ty damn near confirmed that shit.

Whatever the case was, I spoiled the twins endlessly. I guess that was when my relationship started getting fucked up. The more time I spent with the girls, the less time I spent with Milagros. There were times that I damn near had to beg her to do shit for them because I had other things to do. I needed to get my woman back on track.

Right when I was about to talk to her about it, she began to act right. That was a good thing...

Milagros surprised the hell out of me when I asked her to take the girls to their appointment that they had scheduled for the next morning. Normally she would fuss me out, huff and puff before she agreed to it. I didn't think anything of it though because with the amount of time she spent with the girls I was starting to think they finally grew on her.

She was drunk as shit when I asked her too so maybe that played a factor is things but so what. I woke her up that morning before leaving out because I had some business to handle. Word on the street was that La'Karata had been spotted out West near one of my houses and she indeed had a child with her. I needed to find out about her and him.

I made it out West in no time seeing as I was flying down the expressway like I always did. I went to my meeting and then hit a few blocks and hollered at some of my workers. I knew I was the boss but I still needed those little niggas to see that I wasn't above trappin' with their asses. I knew how to get down too.

When I was out in front of the trap on Kimball Avenue, I heard her voice. She was screaming at a little boy for running ahead of her.

"*Junior*! Junior, got damn it I know you hear me. I told yo lil ass about running off on me like that. You can't be doing that shit. I should whoop yo ass right now in front of everybody."

"You ain't gonna whoop shit!" the little boy responded and I chuckled.

I stood back watching their interaction before making my presence known. I was also waiting to see if the little boy would turn around so I could get a good look at him. After a few minutes of stalling around, I decided to break that shit up.

"Hey La, what's good with you? Long time no see huh? And who's this you got with you?"

The little boy turned to look at me and I almost shit myself. He looked just like me! How the fuck was I supposed to explain this shit to Milagros. Shit, La had some serious explaining to do as well. Before I could say anything else the little boy spoke.

"Hello Sir. My name is Amon Rivers Jr. I was born May 23, 2007. I am eight years old."

"Well it's nice to meet you Amon Rivers Jr. Guess what my name is?"

"That's easy. Your name is Amon Rivers Sr. and you are my father. I know because we look just alike. I have a picture of you beside my bed! My mother told me you were my father after I kept asking about you. She told me that eventually I would get to meet you."

"You seem to be a really smart young man. And you're right, we do look alike. Would you like to hang out with me some time?"

He looked over at his mom. "Ohhhh can I Mommy?"

"Junior let me talk with your father for a few minutes and then I'll make a decision ok. Just hurry up and get to grandma's house like I told you."

"Ok Mommy." Junior said before taking off towards the apartment building his grandma stayed in.

"So La were you ever going to tell me?"

"Man Amon I ain't tryna hear that shit. You told me you wanted a DNA test and a bunch of other shit. How do you think I felt knowing the one nigga that I cared about thought I was a ho' like the bitch he had before me? It was like you were treating me like shit because of what Ty did and I didn't deserve none of that. When you told me to get out your car that day I decided that I'd just raise my baby myself because I didn't have time for games."

"Naw fuck that La. You wrong and you know it. I wouldn't let my seed go without for nothing. You got my lil nigga out here looking like a lil homeless kid. You knew good and damn well how to get ahold of me and I would've taken care of him."

"Well now you know so now you can. You can spend as much time with him as you want but I don't want my son around that bitch Milagros. She already threatened me and had Ty killed. I don't like that ho' from how she took you from me either. She ain't about to take my son from me though."

"Look Milagros ain't got shit to do with this and she damn sho' didn't have Ty killed! Keep her name out ya mouth and show some fucking respect. Ain't shit changed about me, ya dig? I'll still fuck you up."

"Yeah, yeah whatever Amon. By the way, he's just like you ya know. He's smarter than I ever was or am. He's a genius. Certified, just like his daddy. That's just in case you were wondering if he was yours or not. That along with the fact that he's a spitting image of you should be DNA enough for yo ass. Now if you don't mind, I have to go tend to my, oops, I mean our son."

I didn't say shit else as La'Karata walked off. All I could think about was what the hell I was going to tell Milagros. She was already feeling some type away about twins that weren't mine and I was raising them. I knew she would go ape shit once I told her I had a son; Especially by La'Karata. The last thing I needed was a fight so I would keep it to myself for now.

<u>Milagros</u>

That was the longest week of my life. I had been checking my messages on my blow up cell for the past three days hoping the results would be in early.

"Babe, your cell is going off nonstop!" I fussed as his ringtone threw my thoughts off. "You want me to bring it to you?"

"Yeah," Amon yelled out from the bathroom.

Just as I reached for it a text came through.

"Call me, La"

"I know this better not be that bitch La'Karata!" I wondered silently. "How the fuck this ho' get the number and why does Amon have the shit stored in his fucking phone?" Oh, I was hotter than fish grease!

I had been low key looking for that bitch for the past few years. I was still salty with that ho' for talking shit and I didn't get to serve her ass with a good old fashioned beat down.

"Here," I huffed as I tossed it to him.

Amon looked at the screen and up at me.

"What?"

"What?" I snapped and rolled my eyes as I slammed the door behind me. "Stankin' ass, spray when you're done!"

It wasn't a good time to confront Amon about La'Karata. I wanted to keep my focus on the paternity test. I just had to know if my man had been lying to me for all those years.

"Why you always got a nasty ass attitude Milly?" he asked as he stepped into my personal space.

"Why you always hiding shit Amon?"

"Here you go!"

"You right!" I spat as I grabbed my purse and headed out. "Here the fuck I go!"

Amon didn't even try to stop me. I assumed he just wanted to call the trick La'Karata back. "He better talk why he can because when I find the bitch she's dead!"

I hopped in the car and hit the highway. I went straight over to my cousin Liana's house. I was ready to drink and hit some bud. I rarely smoked but I wanted to be prepared for the phone call I had been waiting for.

"Girl, you sure have been coming over here a lot!" Liana clowned as she passed me the blunt as soon as I walked into the door.

"Hush I'm going through some shit right now!" I blurted out nearly busting myself up.

"What?" Liana questioned in disbelief. "The one person I know that always seems to have everything under control? What is it prima?"

"Nothing," I answered trying to downplay it.

"Nothing is a lie!" Liana snapped. "We tell each other everything, so out with it!"

I took a deep sigh and stared at her strangely wondering if I could trust her fully. We had always been so close, but now that we were older I rarely shared my deepest secrets.

"Well," I started before I was interrupted by the ringing of my cell.

I held my finger in the air motioning her to hold on for a moment. I then connected the call and listened carefully. When the woman was finished and hung up, I was still clinching the phone tightly.

"What is it?" Liana snapped. "What the hell is going on Milagros?"

"The twins are really Amon's," I mumbled feeling sick to my stomach.

"What?"

"Yeah," I whispered with tears of betrayal invading my eyes.

My heart hurt deeply and all I could do to make it better was to hurt Amon back. I needed to plan carefully.

"What are you going to do prima?" Liana started. "Have you even signed the papers to legally adopt the twins? Does Amon know that you can't have kids?"

I didn't want to hear shit that was falling from my cousin's mouth. Everything she was saying was a harsh reality that I wasn't ready to face. I couldn't lie. The shit was hard...

"No, Amon never even filed the paperwork in the first place for me to sign!" I shot remembering about the whole situation. "Matter of fact, the motherfucker is hiding more than that and I'm going to get to the bottom of the shit!"

"One thing at a time Milagros!" Liana warned. "We have a big family and if you need something taken care of let one of the elders handle the shit."

I needed to handle shit on my own. I didn't need the family up in my business like that. I had a hard enough time keeping everything away from them. If I was going to do something foul to Amon, it had to be inflicted with my own two hands in order for me to feel just satisfaction...

"First I'll confront him about this and then I'll bring that La'Karata shit up to him," I thought aloud as I drank my Hennessey and hit the weed again.

"How about you deal with the shit pertaining to the twins and let me handle the shit with the other chick?" Liana offered. "You don't want one thing to bite you in the ass while taking care of the other!"

We sat there going back and forth about the whole ordeal when Liana asked me what I would do if Amon wanted to leave me.

"Honestly the thought never crossed my mind," I replied truthfully.

"Well you know he takes everything with him if he does right?"

"Everything like what?" I snapped becoming upset.

"The house is in your name, but the other two are in his. You said he has his own account and material things, so consider taking a loss if you two split. Not to mention your reputation will be damaged with the family. Remember, they are all waiting for this relationship to fail. They'll be begging to put his ass six feet under!"

"Whoa," I stopped her. "I hope it doesn't come to all that."

"You have to think about the bigger picture prima. If things are as bad as you are making them out to be, shit is going to hit the fan as soon as you expose his skeletons. Be prepared."

"Naw, he better be prepared!" I warned still sipping on my cup of courage. "I already know for a fact that the twins are his and as soon as I hit him with a copy of the email the lady sent he can't say shit!"

"Oh, he can say a whole lot Milagros! Like I said, be prepared…"

I took my cousin's words to heart and went ahead and gave her the green light to see what was up with La'Karata. She definitely needed to be taken care of.

Until then, I was going to try my damnedest not to bring up my new little discovery. I just prayed that I could hold my tongue…

Amon Rivers

After Milagros stormed out, I stood there for a minute wondering what the fuck was wrong with her before turning my attention to my phone. When I unlocked it, I saw the reason for her immediate attitude. I had gotten a text message from La'Karata. No wonder she was pissed. I would definitely have to make it up to her later. I opened the text to see that what La said was simply for me to call her.

Now given the history with this chick, I could understand why Milagros would get pissed off, especially after she came for both of us. I figured though that with eight years having gone by, Milagros would know where I wanted to be. Hell, I had been with her all this time. Women would always be strange creatures to me. I just shook my head as I dialed La's number.

"Hello," she answered picking up on the third ring.

"Yo La, it's Amon. You said you needed me to call you. What's up?"

"Ok don't take this as I'm trying to start some shit but I think ya girl is on some bullshit."

"Fuck you mean? Man La, I ain't tryna be dealing with no baby mama drama from ya ass."

"Damn nigga didn't I just say I wasn't tryna start anything? A dark colored Crown Vic been following me all damn day. Now I've been back in the city for a month now with no issues but after talking to you I start getting followed. I didn't know if it was your doing or hers, so that's why I hit you up. Your reaction told me that I assumed right by it being her."

"I really don't know what the hell you're talking about but I'll check into it aight? Other than that is my son straight? Does he need anything?"

"No he's good Amon. He just wanted to know when he can spend some time with you."

"Yeah about that. I can come over there and chill with lil man but he can't come here yet."

"And why is that?" La snapped with an attitude.

"Because I haven't told Milagros yet!"

"What? I can't fuckin' believe you Amon! We're hiding our child now, huh? Is that what the fuck we do?" La'Karata screamed out at the top of her fucking lungs.

"Yo man, calm ya lil ass down. I got this and you got a lot of fuckin' nerve talkin' bout hiding our son! Anyway, I'll be by to see him tomorrow. Until then stay y'all asses in the house because if something happens to him then I'm blaming you."

I didn't even bother waiting for a response. I just hung up, got myself together and went to check on the girls. I knew that with all this tension in the house, they would pick up on it. The last thing I needed was for my princesses to be worried about anything. It was my job to worry not theirs. I left out and started towards their adjoining rooms.

I knew that more likely Adora was in Soledad's room. That was just how the girls were. Adora was the loud, obnoxious twin whereas Soledad was the quieter, reserved twin. They had a way of balancing each other out.

I loved those little girls with everything in me. I had started introducing Soledad to the other aspect of my business with simple conversation. I didn't want to introduce her to the gritty side just yet. She surprised me though by having a complete understanding of what I was telling her. She even surprised me when she asked me when I was going to start training her to take over the family business. I laughed only to see that the expression on her face was dead ass serious. It was then that I knew Soledad had what it took to do this; Even at the age of eight...

I walked up on the girls' door and stopped just short of the entrance when I heard the twins talking.

"So big sister, what are we gonna do?" Adora questioned.

"It's simple little sister. We have to get her out of the picture. You know she doesn't like us nor does she hide the disgust she has for us when Daddy isn't around." Soledad replied.

"How we gonna do that though? You know that Daddy loves her."

"But he loves us even more. All we have to do is wait for the right time to expose her for what she really is. Patience is the key little sister. Just be patient and in due time, it will all take care of itself."

I couldn't believe my ears. I wasn't surprised at how intelligent of a conversation they were holding for being only eight years old but I was shocked at the fact that they felt as if Milagros didn't like them. They never even so much as uttered a word about being mistreated by her in any way. The last thing I wanted was to have to choose because Soledad was right. I would chose the girls in a heartbeat.

I decided to not let them know I had overheard their conversation. I would just have to start looking into things myself. I just prayed that they wouldn't do anything to Milagros before I had a chance to handle shit.

"Hey girls. What do you say we go grab some McDonald's and a movie?" I suggested making an entrance.

"Daddy!" they screamed in unison.

They both ran to me and I scooped them up into my arms. I loved those little girls more than my own life. We played around a bit before the girls got their shoes and coats on so we could head out.

While we were riding, I decided to ask them a few questions.

"So girls, how would you feel about having a brother?"

"What? Milagros is pregnant?" Adora snapped with much disdain.

"I guess," Soledad responded.

I could hear the hatred for Milagros in both their voices.

"No Milly isn't pregnant, but can you keep a secret?"

"Yes!" they replied in unison.

"You two have a little brother and soon I'll be taking you both to go meet him. He's only a little younger than you two but you are all the same age. Remember though, this stays between us."

"You got it Daddy." Adora promised with a huge smile on her face.

"No problem Daddy." Soledad replied.

"That's my girls. Now what do you guys want to eat?" I asked pulling up to McDonald's.

After I placed our order, the girls chatted happily. I didn't engage in their conversation. I just watched and listened until our food was ready. I grabbed the tray and followed behind the twins.

As we sat in the play place, I thought about the situation at hand while the girls played and ate. I knew I didn't have anything to worry about when it came to the twins telling Milagros anything about their brother.

They made it clear that they didn't like her. What bothered me was why. I wanted to confront Milagros to see what her problem was but at the same time, I wanted to sit back and check things out for myself.

"We're ready daddy," they sang out in unison. I couldn't help but laugh.

"Alright, let's go girls."

I got the twins in the car and just as I was pulling off, my phone rang. I immediately recognized the number and a smile spread across my face. It was Tina.

I had grown very fond of her since I met her a few years back. She was also a great asset to my empire. I answered happily.

"Hey you. How are things going?"

"I'm doing just fine Amon. How are things with you? How are the girls?"

"I'm ok but I do have some business to discuss with you. Can you drop by if you have the time? And the girls are just fine."

"Daddy is that Ms. Tina?" Soledad asked.

I shook my head yes.

"Hey Ms. Tina!" the girls shouted out in unison once again.

"Hey girls." Tina laughed answering them back. "So what business do we need to discuss Amon?"

"That would be better talked about in person Tina. When do you think you can make it?"

"I'll leave now and can be there in about 40 minutes or so. Is the misses gonna be around? I'd love to finally meet her. We've been doing business for a few years now so I think it's time I meet my other boss, don't you think?"

"Yeah she'll be around Tina and I'd like for you all to meet anyway. I'll see you when you get to my house."

"Ok see you then."

After hanging up with Tina I decided that I would tell her my suspicions about Milagros who I was sure had not made it home yet. After she flew out the house earlier I knew she was probably at Liana's house. She had been spending more and more of her time over there lately. I really didn't mind it until it became a pattern. It was like she would find a reason to pick a fight then fly out the door over there. I didn't think she was cheating on me but if she was there would be hell to pay. That was another thing for another time though because I had more pressing issues to handle.

****

We pulled into the driveway of our home and as I thought, Milagros wasn't home yet. That gave me enough time to send the girls to their rooms and speak with Tina before she arrived.

Right as the twins raced up the stairs, the doorbell rang. I checked the security monitor to see who it was. Noticing it was Tina I quickly went to let her in.

"Hey there Tina. You made it here quickly."

"Well when the boss calls I gotta come right away. Besides, I wanted to see the girls anyway. I came bearing gifts."

"You know they're spoiled enough as it is right? You're just making it worse." I laughed as I called for the twins.

When they reached the top of the steps, they saw Tina with bags in her hands and came barreling down the staircase. Soledad was the first to reach the bottom and ran straight into Tina's open arms. Tina embraced her and spun her in a circle as Adora went through the bags Tina had dropped.

"Sol look! She got us the American Girl dolls we've been asking Daddy for. Tina you're the best!"

Soledad immediately jumped out of Tina's arms and ran to the doll her sister was holding up.

"Thanks so much Tina. You're the best. We love you." The shouted before they retreated back to their rooms.

I was shocked at the girls' reaction to a simple gift from a friend of mine. They never even showed that much appreciation when Milagros did anything for them, but after overhearing them earlier, I understood why which brought my attention back to Tina.

I grabbed her lightly by the elbow and led her to my study. After grabbing a few drinks and taking a seat I got right down to business.

"Well Tina I need you to look into Milagros for me. Lately she's been acting really strange and then I overheard a conversation the girls were having that made me believe she's on some bullshit."

"Overheard the girls say what Amon? I swear if she's trying to hurt them in any way I-"

"Hold on killa," I chuckled. "They didn't say anything about her hurting them in any way but they did say they didn't like her and that she treats them differently when I'm not around. I was always taught that you should listen to what a child has to say about the person you're with because they can see things you can't. I'm going with my girls on this one. I need you to find whatever it is that you can."

"Ok I'm on it boss and Amon?"

"Yes Tina?"

"I'm letting you know now if I find something I don't like then boss or no boss, she's dead."

"You got that Tina."

I was shocked with myself because even I didn't think she would react that way. You could tell her love for the girls was genuine though and I couldn't blame her.

As we sat discussing other business and some things she had been looking into for me, my woman finally decided to show up. She came straight in talking shit.

"Well what do we have here? Who is this woman Amon and why is she in my house looking all chummy with my man?" Milagros slurred.

Before things got out of hand, I jumped up and made the introduction.

"Babe this is Tina. She is the woman I was telling you about that has been helping us on the technical side of things. Remember, I brought her back with me from North Carolina after that situation with Colay, DJ and Marina?"

"Oh yeah, the computer bitch."

"Um excuse you but my name is Tina, thank you. I would like to be referred to by my name and not 'the computer bitch' like you've been referring to me. I don't disrespect you so I expect you not to disrespect me especially when I'm standing right here."

"Hold up one got damn minute. You're in my muthafu-"

"Alright enough! Let's go Milagros. You are embarrassing us both right now. You need to go upstairs while I finish business with Tina. Come on."

I grabbed Milagros and drug her drunk ass up the stairs. I pushed her towards our bedroom door, pissed off like hell. I couldn't believe she acted that way. Tina had done nothing to her and she wanted to show her ass. If she was going to be any queen of mine, then she needed to know how to get her shit together. I pulled her into our room and slammed the door. She was turning into nothing but a big ass drunk and I wasn't feeling that shit.

"What the hell was that Milagros? You had no right to insult the woman that has been keeping us ahead of every federal agency since we met her. You need to get it together ma. That shit wasn't cool."

"Fuck you Amon. I don't know why you're sticking up for her. What, you fucking her?"

"Are you shitting me right now? No I'm not fucking anybody but you but you don't see that shit. Right now you're acting like a little girl with that jealous shit. Green is not a good look on you."

"What the fuck ever! This is my house and I'll act however I want in it. Go back to your computer bitch and leave me be Amon."

I didn't say one word. I just stormed out the room. Had I been paying closer attention I would've noticed Soledad sitting in the hallway in the shadows but I didn't until it was too late. She had hurried into her sister's room. I didn't bother her.

I was beyond pissed at my so-called woman's actions so I headed back downstairs to apologize to Tina for what happened. When

I got to the bottom of the steps I saw Tina gathering her things. I rushed to her.

"I'm so sorry about that Tina. Here, let me walk you out."

"Ok Amon but we'll discuss what I wanna say outside. Last thing I need is for her to come for me again. Then I'd have to slap that bitch."

I followed Tina out the door and proceeded to walk her to her car. When we made it, she popped the locks and we both got in.

"I see what you mean about her behavior now Amon. That woman I met doesn't seem like the woman you described to me. She sounds like her world is tumbling down around her and it has a lot to do with you."

"Thank you for being honest and once again I apologize for her behavior. Now you see why I asked you to check into her and what she's been doing. Something isn't right and it's not sitting well with me. I don't like waiting for the other shoe to drop."

"Understood. I'll get on it as soon as I get home but I meant what I said earlier. If I find anything I don't like I will kill that bitch."

"Understood as well but you need to let me handle her. Last thing I need is for the cartel to come looking for my ass should something happen to her. I have more than just myself to think about now."

"Ok I'll give you that Amon so I'll let you handle it but I want to be there if you need to do anything."

"That's a deal. I appreciate you Tina. Drive safely and let me know you made it home. Have a good night."

I hopped out Tina's car and watched her drive out the long driveway. There was something about that woman that was special but that was a relationship I couldn't partake in. Maybe in another place at another time but right then I had to fix what was going on in my own house.

I went back inside and locked up behind me setting the alarm. I took the stairs two by two hurrying to make it to our bedroom. Milagros was going to tell me something that night.

As I made it to the top of my steps I heard light sobbing coming from Soledad's room. I went to check on my little girl before I handled that half-ass grown woman in my room.

I knocked softly before I heard Adora tell me to come in. As I suspected, Soledad was crying and Adora was consoling her. Adora looked at me with pain in her eyes and it was clear that she was hurting because her twin was. I needed to make them feel better.

"Sol, baby are you ok? Daddy's right here. Tell me what's wrong."

"Daddy why did she treat Ms. Tina that way? That was very, very mean and I didn't like it. I don't like her."

"I don't know why she did that but I'm going to fix that ok? Don't you worry your pretty little head about that. Now wipe those tears and let's get you into bed."

"Ok Daddy."

I tucked the girls in and left back to take care of the matter at hand. When I walked into our room, Milagros was passed out on our bed.

"I am gonna let her sleep it off tonight but tomorrow her ass owes me an explanation."

****

(Soledad)

"You think he bought it Adora?"

"Come on Sol. This is Daddy we're talking about. You know he did." Adora said with a slight giggle.

"Ok so what do you think about what I told you?"

"I say we go to Ms. Tina for help. You know we can't ask Daddy because he'll automatically say no."

"Alright then that's what we'll do. Next time I use Daddy's phone I'll get her number while you distract him."

"Deal big sister. Now come on and let's go to sleep."

Milagros

Things had gotten way out of hand since I had found out about the twins. My emotions were spinning all over the place and I could not control them. That was why I flipped the fuck out when I came home and found Amon in my house with the computer bitch. Yes, I said my fucking house!

I may have been drunk, but I saw the way Tina was eyeing Amon. Even worse, I caught the way he was lusting after her as well. He was becoming way beyond disrespectful and we needed to talk about it before it was unfixable.

"About last night..." I began before Amon cut me off.

"Look, I don't want to wake up arguing about that dumb shit. I said what I had to say last night so leave it alone."

"So what if..."

"Seriously Milly," he went on as he climbed out of the bed and headed for the shower. "I don't want to talk about it."

"Fuck it," I mumbled under my breath as I turned over and pretended to go back to sleep.

I stayed positioned there until Amon was dressed and out of the bedroom. When the door closed lightly behind him, I sat straight up in the bed and listened for the garage to open and then close. After that, I waited five minutes before I hopped up and got myself together.

Checking my cell before I hopped in my ride, I saw that my battery was dead. I plugged it into the outlet and waited for it to power on before I backed out of the driveway. As soon as it did, the alerts began to go off back to back...

"What the hell?" I huffed as I read the first couple of messages from Liana.

She had indeed done some digging and came up with a whole bunch of shit. The information that she had forwarded to me was way more than I expected. It was enough that I had to deal with the twins and now my cousin was telling me that Amon may have a son by that bitch La'Karata. I didn't know what to bust him up about first, or if I even wanted to go through a verbal confrontation. I was debating more on just taking all of them out to eliminate the whole problem...

I decided not to call Liana before going to her house. She had been working from home so I knew that she would be there. She rushed me the moment she opened up the door.

"Did you get my messages?"

"Yes I did."

"I had the La'Karata girl followed and look girl!"

Liana shoved picture after picture into my face. She even had some of Amon with La'Karata and her son. Yes, that little boy was dead on my man.

My rage was out of control and I wasn't thinking clearly when I began barking out threats. I just shouted out the first things that came to mind.

"If the bastard would have married me I could have killed his ass and raised the twins myself for my own reasons. Naw, then Amon wouldn't be here to suffer. I would be the one suffering."

I paced back and forth.

"I should just kill the La'Karata bitch and her illegitimate son! Naw, he would know I had something to do with it."

"Not necessarily Milagros..." Liana interrupted.

"What do you mean?"

"Don't bring up shit about it. Act like you don't know and let me take care of it," she explained. "I will do it when I know you're with Amon. That way he won't suspect you."

"Deal," I chanted. "Take care of it today!"

"You got it prima," Liana promised. "I will text you with an emoji telling you goodnight. When you get that it will mean La'Karata's gone 'nite-nite' for good!"

"And her kid!"

Liana nodded silently and walked me to the door.

On my way back to the house, I sent Amon a text apologizing for how I acted when Tina was there. It hurt my soul to send that damn message because I could care less about the bitch. She was just another distraction for Amon.

Instead of responding in a text, Amon rung my cell. I answered it on the first ring and blew him a kiss.

"I'm sorry baby," I whispered. "I can't even make up an excuse for my behavior lately."

"It's cool," Amon replied hesitantly as if he was not quite buying my lies.

"Well, I wanted to know if you and the twins wanted to have a nice dinner at home tonight. I'll have everything ready by six."

"Okay, we'll be there," he spoke dryly before hanging up.

I knew after our brief conversation that I would have to come much stronger than I had been. I had to find something that would soften him up... and I knew sex wasn't going to do it.

After rushing home, I got the housekeeper Medina to run to the grocery store to pick up all of the girl's favorites. I knew the way to get to Amon was through the twins. I never used them in the past because I tried to stay clear, but now I was face to face with desperate times and they definitely called for desperate measures...

"I will have everything hot and on the table by 6pm ma'am," she assured. "Don't worry about a thing. I know just what the twin's love! They are going to be so happy!"

I shooed her off not wanting to get wrapped up in her joy while I was plotting for me to get my own. Instead, I took my ass upstairs to get all dolled up.

Letting my hair down, I brushed it to the side and allowed my curls to fall on my bare shoulder. My strapless purple gown hugged each and every curve that Amon was so attracted to. I knew just what turned him on and I was prepared to pull out every trick I knew.

****

"Damn, you look good and smell good," Amon complimented as he crept up on me while I was sitting at my vanity fastening my necklace.

"Let me help you," he offered.

I stood up as Amon took me by the hand and admired me. I saw the look in his eyes that I hadn't seen in quite some time. I knew right then I had his ass.

"The girls are downstairs waiting. You know as soon as they smelled the grilled chicken smothered in that white gravy they went crazy."

I smiled even harder knowing that he was falling for my plan... Especially when he clinched my palm and we descended the stairs hand in hand.

My ego was at an all-time high until I walked into the formal dining room of our home. That was when my face dropped. Just the sight of Tina at the table laughing and playing with the girls had me heated.

I bit my tongue and forced a smile while Amon whispered in my ear. "Didn't you want to apologize baby?"

Tightening my grip on his hand, I let up and let go. Then I faced him and nodded affirmatively.

"Oh, hello Tina, forgive me I wasn't expecting you," I blurted out causing Amon to nudge my side. "Oh, and I wanted to apologize for last night. Forgive me please?"

Those words were some of the hardest words I had to allow to fall out of my mouth and the taste was awful. I didn't know how much longer I had to play nice without blowing the fuck up.

Amon pulled out my chair and waited for me to sit down before he helped scoot me close to the table. He then bent down and kissed me on the cheek. "Thank you baby."

"Yeah, yeah," I thought silently and quickly gave him a fake grin.

Right away I noticed the twins taking to Tina. It was like they had known her for years. It instantly got my mind clicking. I needed a drink.

That one drink led to the next and before I knew it dinner was over and I was drunk once again. I was too through. By then everything was irking the hell out of me.

"My daughter's this, my twins that," I complained without barriers. "These are not even your kids and you are going on and on about them. You even got this computer bitch over here talking about they are your daughters!"

Amon jumped up so fast and wrapped his hands around my throat I didn't have an adequate chance to respond.

"Wait, stop!" Tina shouted as she shoved the twins back and came towards us with some papers. "Let her go!"

Amon calmed down and released me as Tina shoved the papers in his face. He took a few seconds to skim them over a couple of times. I had no idea what they were until the interfering bitch spoke again. I was too busy trying to catch my breath. I could not believe that fool put his fucking hands on me!

"They are your twins Amon!" Tina explained as she pointed to the top of the documents that he was holding tightly.

Lifting his head up slowly, Amon gave me the look of death. "You knew about this? Did you do this?"

Before I could answer him truthfully and admit that I knew about his son with La'Karata, my cell vibrated inside my hidden pocket on my dress. I drew it out and saw that it was a message from Liana.

"Goodnight prima..."

I knew what that meant. That was just the first phase of my plan.

"Just wait and see what I have in store for you Amon!" I thought silently as I ran from the room and headed upstairs.

As badly as I wanted to leave the house, I knew I couldn't. My whereabouts had to be accounted for if and when I got questioned about the murders of La'Karata and her son...

****

(*Soledad*)

"Don't you just love it when a great plan comes together Adora?" I teased as soon as Tina and Daddy sent us to our room.

"I don't know why she even had to question if he was our father or not?" she replied with a peculiar expression. "Do you think there is more to our mother's death than dad let on?"

"All I know is that he is our father and he loves us more than anything in this world!" I assured Adora. "Let's not worry about anything else okay?"

"Okay Sis," Adora promised. "I love him more than anything too."

"Me too Sis," I confessed. "Me too..."

Amon Rivers

Just when I thought everything was getting back good between Milagros and I, she does some stupid shit. After her outburst at dinner and Tina showing me those papers, I didn't know how to react other than the way I did. I grabbed Milagros by her throat and was ready to crush her esophagus when Tina pulled me off of her. I looked around wild eyed because I forgot that the twins were in the room.

After sending the girls upstairs, I turned back to Milagros to see that she had gone up there as well. I then followed Tina outside to her car. She climbed in sat next to me as I looked at the paperwork again. Right there on the first page in black and white it said that I was 99.98% the father of Adora and Soledad.

"How is this even possible?"

Ty's due date did not add up plus I found out she was messing with ol boy. I just couldn't wrap my head around this shit.

I was in a daze when I felt Tina's hand on mine. Despite what just went down, she was still there. There was definitely something special about her. As far as Milagros was concerned, our relationship was just about over. I just wanted to extract myself from this situation as smoothly as possible because of who she was. Last thing I needed was for her family to come for me.

"Amon, are you going to be ok? I can stay if you need me to."

"No I'm not ok but I will be Tina. Thanks so much for finding out what she was up to. I really appreciate it."

"No problem boss. You know I'd do anything for you and the girls."

Before I could say anything else Tina leaned over and kissed me lightly on the lips. Just that small, innocent kiss set my body ablaze. In that moment I wanted her and didn't care that Milagros was in the house, but I knew the girls were as well so I had to stop myself. Trust me I did not want to! Hell, I was hard as a brick, but I still managed to pull away.

"I'm sorry Tina. I got ahead of myself there."

"It's on Amon. I wanted it more than you know."

Tina winked at me before getting out the car and coming around to the driver's side where I was sitting. I watched her walk with longing in my eyes and I got out to get a quick hug. I wanted that woman something terrible but I would have to put that on hold until I handled my business with Milagros.

I then made my way to the door. Soon as I got inside heard the car pull off and knew that Tina was gone.

I wasn't ready just yet to confront that woman upstairs so I sat drinking by myself at the dining room table looking over the paperwork once more.

****

(*Soledad*)

Adora had fallen asleep on my bed so I left her there and went to use the bathroom. On my way across the hall I heard Milagros on the phone so I decided to eavesdrop on her conversation. Even though I couldn't hear what the other person was saying, I wanted to hear what she had to say in case it was something I could use against her.

When I made it to the door, I peeked in to see her back was to me. I wondered whom she was talking to. Whoever it was, she was barking orders at them. I listened on until I heard my mother's name.

"I didn't give a fuck about that Ty bitch and I don't give a fuck about that computer bitch either. She has to go. I don't need no bitch thinking they can take my man from me. Ty tried that shit and you see how she ended up. I'm just glad that Amon never put two and two together."

No this bitch didn't! I know my ears were not failing me. I was so mad and I knew I should not have been swearing but I could not control my anger.

A rage took over my tiny body and I made a vow right then and there that I would put Milagros six feet under if it was the last thing I did.

****

(*Amon*)

I must have drunk about six cups of Hennessey before pulling myself from the table. I felt slightly dizzy when I stood up so I leaned on the counter for a minute. I steadied myself and climbed the stairs. I thought maybe I had one too many to drink because when I reached the top on the stairs I saw Soledad standing outside my bedroom door. I shook my head to see if maybe I was seeing and when I looked up again she was gone. Yeah, I was seeing shit.

I stumbled to my door and caught the tail end of Milagros on her phone. I heard her say La'Karata's name and wondered what that was about.

There was no sense in beating around the bush. The shit was almost over anyway. I took a step in her direction and spun her around to face me.

"Who's that on the phone Milly? And why are you talking about La'Karata? No one has seen her in years."

"I wasn't talking about that bitch. Your drunk ass just heard whatever you wanted to hear."

"I know what I heard and I heard you say her name as sure as I hear you talking to me now. Why you bringing up old shit for? You got me, not anyone else so why you worried about my old bitches?"

Milagros didn't say shit to me she just turned back around and tossed her phone on the bed. She kicked off her shoes and slid her dress down her fit body. My dick immediately bricked up but I would not let him control my actions that night.

I counted to ten in my head and blew a breath out. Sex was not going to fix any problem we had.

Suddenly, Milagros turned towards me with a smile on her face but once she saw my expression she knew something was wrong. She sucked her teeth at me and I just shook my head at her.

Walking past Milagros, I climbed into the bed with my clothes still on. I turned my back to her as I felt her get on her side of the bed. Before I knew it, she had slithered her ass over to my side, but I was not having it. Next, I felt her hands slide up my chest. That shit did not work either. I shook her right on off.

"Damn Amon, what the fuck?"

"Fuck you mean? I ain't going there with you tonight Milagros."

"Oh I'm Milagros now?"

"You damn right. After the shit you pulled tonight I don't wanna deal with ya ass. And tell me this, when the fuck was you gonna tell me that you knew the twins were mine?"

"Fuck you Amon! I know you knew that shit from jump!"

"Don't turn this shit around on me Milagros. When the fuck was you gonna tell me, huh? You went and got a test on the girls even after I kept telling your ass I wasn't their father. I was going off what I found out about their mother but you just couldn't leave well enough alone, could you?"

"I did what I had to do Amon and I'm not ashamed of it. I knew you were lying to me the whole time."

"*I wasn't fuckin' lying*! I didn't know, especially after finding out her due date. Why can't you just fucking believe me?"

"What the fuck ever Amon. I don't believe you, especially about the ho's you used to mess with. Like why is La'Karata texting you when we haven't heard nothing from her ass in years huh? Explain that shit!"

"How the fuck would I know? I haven't heard from her ass in forever and day but all of a sudden she hits me up and that's my fault? Get the fuck outta here!"

"How the fuck she get your number Amon? We got that shit changed a long time ago!"

I couldn't take anymore of her shit so I got up and stormed out the room. I was going to sleep in the guest room that night because if I didn't I was sure to slap the piss out of her.

I peeked in on the girls and saw they were sleeping so I continued to the next room. Once I got inside, I didn't bother with the light. I threw myself on the bed and passed out. I didn't even feel it when someone when probing in my damn pockets...

****

(*Soledad*)

I waited until Daddy had passed out and I was sure he was sleeping before I snuck his phone out his pants. I had to get Tina's number so I could call her and tell her what I heard. I swear if Tina told me that Milagros had anything to do with my mother being killed then she was dead for sure. I would have to wait patiently to pull it off but I would avenge my mother's death with everything in me...

Milagros

Amon thought his ass was slick with that La'Karata shit, but when I busted his ass up, he was speechless. I couldn't help but talk shit, only not enough for him to know I had something to do with her and her son's death.

"Sorry, but the bitch had to go!" I laughed as I cut on the news to see what I could find out.

After watching an hour-long segment, I came up with nothing. I couldn't understand it. Amon and the girls were already gone, so I picked up the phone and dialed my cousin Liana. I had to find out what was going on.

"What's up prima?"

"What's the word?"

"Come over here Milagros," Liana spoke in a shaky voice. "I got some fire."

"I'm on my way," I promised as I snatched up my handbag and proceeded out to the garage.

I hopped in the Benz and started it up. I couldn't for the life of me figure out what could have happened... Especially after I received the text letting me know that the shit was taken care of.

I shook my head and stayed stressed out during my entire ride over to my cousin's house. I jumped out of my car and damn near broke my neck climbing the stairs in my heels.

"Bam, bam, bam"

I beat on the door hard to rush my cousin to open that motherfucker. I was anxious to hear what went wrong. Liana's face told it all.

"What happened?"

"Prima, we got her. She's dead, but the little boy survived. Apparently, they shot up his bed but he was found hiding in the closet after the fact. The authorities said that the boy got a good look at the shooter and they just posted a composite photo of our cousin Juan! Tío has already sent him back home so he should be safe, but the boy is still alive."

That was the entire point of taking La'Karata out. I wanted her son out of the picture!

"Well after what you say that you and Amon are going through, it shouldn't matter one way or the other," Liana smirked as she fired up some bomb and tried to pass it to me.

I slapped that shit out of her hand and onto the floor. "That wasn't the fuckin' plan and don't you worry about what the hell I'm going through with Amon. His ass is going to get his in just time!"

Liana gave me the look of death and I paid her no mind. She knew how I got down so she kept it on a calm level.

"Well do you want me to have the kid taken out still?"

"Fuck it and fuck Amon! You know what? Just fuck everything!" I shouted out in frustration, snatched my keys and got to stepping.

When I got in my car, I had to sit there for a while to gather my thoughts. All my plans were falling apart. Amon was ready to call it quits. He went from having no kids to having three and I couldn't give him one! "Shit is not supposed to go like this!"

My heart was aching and I didn't know how to handle it. It was my first time truly being in love and now it was about to be over. That was something I couldn't swallow. I just couldn't...

After taking several deep breaths, I stuck the key in the ignition and started my ride up. I shifted the gear into drive and slowly pulled away from the curbside. I had nobody to talk to and nowhere to go but home.

Once I arrived, I noticed that Amon was still gone and the girls hadn't gotten home from school. I took advantage of the alone time and took a hot bath and took a sleeping pill.

I prayed that I didn't wake up until the next morning. I wasn't ready to deal with Amon...

****

I was awakened in the wee hours of the morning to Amon's cell going off. I wasn't sure what time it was because it was still dark outside. I was too busy trying to play sleep once again.

The house was so quiet that I could hear the entire conversation. I couldn't believe my ears...

"Hello?" Amon whispered groggily.

"Dad, this is me!"

I could hear a young boy talking.

"It couldn't be!" I thought to myself as I listened in a little closer.

"Where are you? Where is your mom?"

Amon began to stir and eventually slid out the bed. He kept his voice low, crept into the bathroom and quietly closed the door. Next, he turned on the water to drown out his talking.

Easing my body up without making a peep, I tiptoed to the door so I could hear.

"What happened? Where are you?"

There was a pause then I heard the toilet flush. Several seconds passed before Amon spoke again.

"Don't be scared son. I'm about to come get you."

I listened carefully as the boy gave him the address. Amon repeated it.

"What the fuck?" I thought silently as I rushed and jumped back in the bed and closed my eyes.

It was hard as hell to lay there and not say a word. It was even more difficult to stay silent and not say shit about my man admitting that he had a kid with La'Karata.

I waited patiently for him to leave the house before I got up, got dressed and followed behind him. It was as easy as pie since I had the location. That gave me time to give him a head start.

After entering the address into my GPS, I took my time getting to my destination. I had no idea where it was I was going to until I saw the name on the building. It was Child Protective Services.

Finding Amon's whip parked in front, I decided to position my car a few spots back and get out. I wanted to be close enough to hear and see what was going on. So much for that...

After waiting for more than a half an hour, I opted on going inside. That didn't work, hell, the damn door was locked and you had to ring to get in after hours.

"What the hell am I gonna do now?" I contemplated quickly.

Not swiftly enough because when I completed my thought, I glanced through the glass and saw Amon coming out of a room holding a little boy's hand. He was dead on him.

Ducking back behind the partial wall, I stayed still until they came out and went to the car. Amon had his arm around the boy's shoulder and seemed to be comforting him.

"Everything is going to be okay Son. I'm going to bring you to my house and we'll figure this out."

"Will you stay with me dad?"

"Yes son, I will always be here for you..."

Amon's words traveled off as I lost it. I stomped my ass right on over there and acted a gotdamn fool! I didn't give a fuck!

Amon Rivers

Shit was all-bad with me and Milagros.

"How could she lie to me like that?"

That was what I was thinking as I sped to get my son. All I knew was that he needed me and I needed to get to him.

When I pulled up to the building there was a small group gathered. I squeezed through the sea of people so that I could get in and see my son. With no luck, I went to ask the nearest officer about his whereabouts. He immediately escorted me around as the other cops quickly cleared the area.

Once I entered the building and saw Junior, I could tell that something bad had happened. He was sitting in the hallway on the couch covered in a blanket crying his eyes out.

"Son, are you ok?"

"Daddy! You came. I didn't think you would come."

"I told you I was on my way. You never have to worry about me never coming when you need me, you hear me?"

He just shook his head yes as his grip on me got tight as hell. I turned to the officer that was watching him and asked a few questions.

"Where is his mother and what exactly happened?"

"Sir, let me get someone that could help you better."

The officer walked off towards the back of the office and came back with a stocky looking man. He hurried over to me and stuck his hand out.

"Morning. My name is Detective Watson. I'm the homicide detective that will be handling this case."

"Excuse me? Homicide? What exactly happened?"

"Well it looks as though someone broke into this woman's apartment. It appeared that there was a struggle and the older Ms. Johnson lost her life in the hallway. We found the younger Ms. Johnson near one of the bedrooms in just as bad a condition as her mother. I'm sorry to be the bearer of bad news Sir." He explained holding out some pictures for me to look at. I did so, nodded and handed them right back.

"Can you tell me where you're taking the bodies so that way I can give them a proper burial?"

"Yes Sir. Here's my card and if you give me a call in the next 24 hours I'll have everything you need then."

"Thank you so much Detective Watson. Am I free to go with my son?"

"Yes Sir but I do need you to bring him down to the station later today so we can ask him a few questions. We didn't want to ask him anything without a parent or guardian present."

"I appreciate that. You don't find too many police officers who would do that nowadays."

After that, I ushered my son out the door and down the steps to my car. Just when shit couldn't get any worse I saw Milagros. Last thing I needed was a scene but I knew she was about to make one.

"So you ran outta our house at four in the damn morning to go get this bitch's kid? Another kid you probably don't even know is yours or not and all because you wanna be Captain Save-A-Ho'."

"He is my fuckin' son! I know that to be a fact but while you out here asking me questions let me ask you something. Where the fuck are my daughters?"

It immediately registered on her face that she had left my girls home alone. It took everything in me not to catch a case out there. I wanted to beat her ass badly but I did not need the jail time.

I made sure Junior was strapped in before pulling off and leaving Milagros standing there stuck on stupid. I raced back towards my house to get back to my daughters. Shit had just went from zero to one hundred real quick.

****

I pulled up in front of my house twenty-five minutes later pissed off and hoping that the girls were ok. I picked up my sleeping son and rushed to my front door.

When I walked in something felt off. I laid Junior down on the couch and ran upstairs looking for the girls.

When I saw that they weren't in their rooms I started shouting their names. When they didn't answer I started to panic. I swore right then that if something happened to my daughters then I would kill Milagros and deal with the consequences later.

She walked in the door moments later to me shouting for the girls.

"What the fuck are you shouting for Amon? The girls are fine. They should be in their rooms."

I went flying down the stairs and snatched Milagros up by her neck.

"Bitch, my daughters are not in their rooms or this house. You left them alone. So help me God, if something happened to them you're dead!"

I dropped her ass and left her catching her breath while I almost lost mine. My girls were gone and I felt like my heart had broken because I didn't know where they were.

I searched the house again before making a call to the one person who could help me with my problem.

****

(Soledad)

I waited until I heard both Daddy and Milagros leave this morning before getting out of bed. Thank God we had a maid Medina who lived with us because Milagros obviously forgot about my sister and I as she went to follow behind my daddy.

I crept downstairs to grab the house phone so I could call Tina. I dialed her number and anxiously waited for her to answer. She picked up on the fourth ring.

"Hello, who is this?"

"Ms. Tina, it's Soledad. I need your help."

"Oh my God honey, it's five in the morning. Are you and your sister ok? Where's your daddy?"

"That's why I'm calling you. Something happened and Daddy had to leave out. Milagros didn't even bother with us because she followed right behind Daddy when he left."

"What? She left y'all alone?"

"We're not alone, the maid is here. But anyways, I needed your help because I overheard her on the phone saying something about my mom and I think she killed her. Can you help me?"

"I'm on my way. Keep the phone next to you and stay where you are. Don't answer the door until I call you and tell you I'm in the front."

"Ok and Ms. Tina?"

"Yes baby girl?"

"Please hurry."

****

(Amon)

I pulled out my phone and called Tina. If anybody could find my girls it was her. I dialed her number and waited patiently for her to answer. It seemed like she was waiting for me to call because she answered up on the first ring.

"Amon, oh my God. Is everything ok? When the girls called me I-"

"The girls are with you?"

"Yes. Soledad called me and said both you and Milagros were gone. I rushed right over there. What the hell is going on?"

"I'll tell you when you get here. I need a favor too."

"Anything Amon, you name it."

"I need you to take my son with you when you leave."

"OK, I will. I'm on my way."

I took a seat next to Junior, who was now awake. I assured him that everything was okay. Just then Milagros walked in.

I got up and walked my son into the family room. What I had to say did not need to be heard by Junior's ears.

After getting him situated, I went back in the kitchen. "This bitch better have some good answers for the questions I'm about to shoot at for her, otherwise that's her ass!"

<u>Milagros</u>

I didn't even think about leaving the twins by themselves until Amon busted me up about it. To be honest, those little sneaky ass girls were a lot smarted than he was giving them credit for so I couldn't understand what the big deal was.

Feeling just a twinge of guilt, I hurried behind Amon to check on the girls. By the time I got there, he was already screaming and acting a damn fool. I rushed right in and pretended to help him look.

After a few minutes, I retreated to the bedroom. I rushed my ass to the cart and poured a stiff one.

"Damn, the only man I ever loved has three fucking kids and I can't even give him one!" I reminded myself repeatedly. The shit was killing me slowly...

I cried on the inside as the tears fought to get out. I didn't want to cry. I wanted it to be like it was in the beginning, when Amon and I were actually happy. I wanted my man back but there was no way that I could accept him with his ready-made family. That shit hurt too much.

I could not see myself playing 'mommy' day in and day out to some kids that were not even my own. I had been doing that shit for the past eight years and I couldn't do it another damn day.

It tore up my every being to watch my man love and nurture the twins for a few good reasons. Number one, he grew a bond with them that wound up being tighter than the one we had established. Number two; I couldn't watch Amon interacting with the kids knowing that I could never give him one. That surely made me feel less than a woman each and every day. Number three, I couldn't love them knowing I killed their mother.

Facing the harsh reality, I picked up my glass, filled it and took it to the face for the fourth time straight. My head was already spinning.

Catching myself, I sat down on the bed to calibrate my bearings. Once I did I heard talking downstairs. I listened a little closer once I heard Tina's voice.

"Damn, after all the shit this motherfucker don' put me through? He's still gonna bring the bitch up in the house?"

Pumping myself up to become more irate, I staggered over to the closet and started going through my boxes. "Where is it?"

Finally, after scrambling to the back behind my dresses, I discovered the set of blue boxes. I went directly to the second one from the bottom.

Pushing all the others to the side, I opened my special package up and found my chrome handgun inside. It had been a gift from my late uncle. I always kept it unlocked and loaded for easy access.

As I rose to my feet, I took a deep breath and placed the weapon to my lips. I puckered up and kissed the barrel of the gun.

"This is for you Tío," I whispered. "I know you didn't like his ass no way..."

Turning around, I slowly stepped towards the bedroom door and slipped into the brightly lit hallway. I had to stand there for several seconds in order to adjust my vision.

Right as I was about to make my way down the stairs, I heard Tina's voice again. Although she spoke in a low tone, I could understand her clearly.

I crouched down on the floor and peered through the cherry wood railing. I could not risk the chance at anyone seeing me until I wanted them to.

"I have to go to the bathroom right quick," Tina whispered.

"Okay, I'm about to get the kids in the car and get them situated. I need to make sure the girls got everything I told them to pack." Amon explained in a low voice. "Hurry and be careful before Milagros comes down here acting a damn fool. I want to leave as peacefully as possible."

"What the fuck?" I thought silently as I clinched the gun even tighter than before. "His ass is gonna go peacefully alright! All of those bastards!"

I was becoming more heated by the minute and could not contain my anger. I'm not sure if I even wanted to. I was at a point in my life where I was just like, "fuck it! Fuck everything!" I felt as if I had nothing to lose. To be honest... I didn't.

"Bitch you come up in my house and take my family away?" I slurred and held the gun out towards Tina. "You hear me computer bitch?"

"Put the gun down Milagros," Tina requested calmly with her arms raised high.

"Bitch please," I huffed still aiming my weapon directly at her chest. "You don't run shit up in here!"

"I'm just leaving..." Tina replied as she slowly inched towards the front door.

That was when I noticed she had the twin's backpacks in her hand. I knew right then that the girls had been with her. She had definitely gotten closer to the twins than I thought. That did nothing but push me over the edge.

"Amon get the fuck in here!" I shouted as I let a round off in the ceiling.

Hell, I needed to get his attention. I wanted him to come rushing in just to see his reaction.

"Five, four, three..." I counted as I pretended to get ready to fire my gun at Tina.

"What the fuck?" Amon yelled and then stop dead in his tracks as I shifted the gun towards him.

I waved it motioning him to join Tina's punk ass. He skedaddled his right on over there and took her in his arms. That was all the confirmation I needed.

"You two sorry motherfuckers deserve each other! After all I've done for you Amon? This is how you repay me?"

"Milly put the gun down," Amon insisted with one hand up and the other still around Tina.

"Then y'all wanna play me in my own shit?"

I could feel the sweat trickle down from my armpit to my hip. Next, my arm began to shake.

"I see you don't want to do it Milly," Amon whispered with a soft look in his eyes.

"Get the fuck back! I'm done with you! I'm done with all of this!"

"No! Don't do it Milly!" Amon hollered out blocking my shot from piercing Tina.

"Oh, I see you're just gonna stand there and protect this bitch? This is our home and you let this bitch come up in here and destroy what we've worked so hard to build? I don't understand you Amon and right now none of it matters. Just say your last goodbyes because both of you are going straight to hell."

"What about the kids?" Tina pleaded. "They need their dad!"

"I guess then you'll rest a little easier then."

"What the fuck?"

"I'll take those little bastards and send them down right after you!"

I tightened my grip on the gun and squeezed a couple of times. Nothing happened. I checked the safety and attempted to fire my weapon again.

"Are you looking for these?" Soledad questioned as she entered the house and neared her father. She then held out her hand revealing a few bullets.

"Well I'll be damned..."

<u>Soledad</u>

After hearing all the screaming and yelling plus a gunshot, I had to go check on my daddy. I calmed Adora and Junior down and told them I would be right back. Adora was immediately peaceful but it took a little longer with Junior.

Adora pulled him over to her and wrapped her arms around him assuring our little brother that things would be ok. I kissed them both on the cheek and crept back over to the front door.

I heard Milagros ranting and raving about killing my daddy and Ms. Tina. What she did not know was that nothing was going to happen. After I had called Ms. Tina to come get me, Adora and I had enough time to snoop around in their bedroom. I found a couple blue boxes hidden behind some dresses that belonged to Milagros. In one of the boxes was a chrome handgun. I did not know how to shoot a gun just yet but I knew how to get on Youtube. I found out how to load and unload a gun and that was just what I did.

I got all the bullets out the clip except the one in the chamber. I did not know about that one until I heard the shot. That was what startled me.

It was that psycho Milagros. She was the dumb one that dispersed a piece of hot lead in the house.

I peeped in to see my daddy standing in front of Ms. Tina and Milagros telling him that she was gonna kill us all. There was just one problem with that; she was out of ammunition. It sure was stupid of her for not checking before she went on her rampage.

I walked in and made my presence known.

"Looking for these?" I asked holding my hand out to show the bullets I took earlier.

"You little bitch!" Milagros shouted as she lunged after me.

I moved to the left before she could grab me and that was when Ms. Tina grabbed her by the arm, spun her around and punched her dead in the face. I wanted to laugh so badly, but I held it in.

"That's for calling me the computer bitch." She yelled at Milagros.

Milagros lay on the floor calling out my daddy's name and telling him how much she loved him. What she showed was not love. How she acted was not love. I may have only been eight years old, but I knew that love did not make you kill people to get what you wanted. It made me shudder to even think that had I not found that gun she may have really killed us all. Thank God, that did not happen.

Once Daddy got Ms. Tina and me into the car, we drove away from the house my sister and I had lived in all our lives. It was never our home.

"Hopefully daddy will take us some place new and we could start over; maybe even with Ms. Tina as our new mommy."

Both Adora and I loved her, so I was sure Junior would too. I would just have to get used to having a little brother but I was certain that it would not be a problem.

We hit the expressway and for the first time since leaving Milagros' house, I let go of the breath I was holding. Junior had fallen asleep but Adora was still wide-awake. She reached over and grabbed my pinky with hers before smiling at me. I smiled back and turned to the window lost in my thoughts. I knew that it was not the end of Milagros and all her issues.

I knew that she would be back. By that time, I would be older and ready for her.

There was only thing that was on my mind at that moment and it was revenge. I needed to obtain it not only for my twin and myself but for my mother, my brother's mother and my daddy as well.

That night a fire was lit inside of me. It was the time in life that a monster had been created and her name was Soledad Amada Rivers!

To Be Continued...

Join our mailing list to get a notification when Leo Sullivan Presents has another release!

Text **LEOSULLIVAN** to 22828 to join!

To submit a manuscript for our review, email us at leosullivanpresents@gmail.com